MUST LOVE PETS

Kitten Chaos

MUST LOVE PETS

Kitten Chaos

Saadia Faruqi

SCHOLASTIC INC.

ISBN 978-1-338-78345-2

10 9 8 7 6 5 4 3 2 1 22 23 24 25 26

Printed in the U.S.A. 40

First printing 2022

Book design by Yaffa Jaskoll

For Cleopatra

I miss you, kitty cat

CHAPTER 1

"What's your favorite animal in the whole universe?" Olivia asks me dreamily.

"A dog, obviously," I reply, my eyes closed. "Like that's even a question."

She's asked me this before, lots of times. It's our favorite topic of conversation. We're in our neighborhood park, lying flat on a picnic table with our legs dangling down the sides. I'm in the middle. My best friend, London, is on my left side. Our new friend, Olivia—who moved to California a week ago—is on my right. All I can see is the blue sky above me, with puffy white clouds and a tiny airplane.

What a perfect way to spend summer break.

Our plan: to have the Most Awesome Summer Ever, full of food and fun and animals. Lots and lots of animals.

I can't believe that fifth grade is over, and so many exciting things have already happened. It's all thanks to our new pet-sitting business, Must Love Pets. Last week, we took care of our first client, Sir Teddy, an adorable golden retriever belonging to our neighbor Mrs. Jarrett. Sir Teddy is my dream pet, but he's also a devious escape artist. He made my little brother, Amir, sneeze and my grandfather Dada Jee super annoyed, and finally he got lost. Since we're amazing pet sitters, we organized a neighborhood search party and found him.

And then the three of us had our first ever sleepover, so I guess everything turned out pretty perfect. Right?

Right.

"Your mom still won't get you a dog, Imaan." This is from London, who's known me (and my mom) since we were in preschool. She could be right. Mama has told me forty-four times that we will absolutely not be getting a pet. Ever.

That's not going to stop me from trying, though. "That's why we started Must Love Pets, remember?" I say cheerfully. "To show my mom how responsible I am."

"You're so responsible," Olivia says in a soothing voice. "Who would doubt you?"

I giggle. "Mama. And Dada Jee." Then my smile fades a little. "And maybe even me sometimes."

London turns to look at me. "We don't doubt you," she says seriously. "We know you can do it. By the time summer ends, we'll have taken care of so many pets your mom will call you Miss Responsible."

I give her a grateful look. London is always on my side, no matter what. "Thanks," I say, trying to get my cheerfulness back. Sometimes I feel sad for no reason, like when I remember my dad, who died of brain cancer when I was little, or when I think of that perfect dog just waiting for me to bring him home. But the sadness never lasts too long. My friends are always there to push me back into happiness.

Olivia nudges me from the other side. "Imaan the Responsible. Like a knight in medieval times."

I pretend to groan. "Seriously? That's the worst name ever for a knight in shining armor."

"What? Being responsible is super important."

She's right. I try to be the best big sister, the best granddaughter, and the best daughter a mother could have, even though Mama can be annoyingly strict sometimes. I clean up every day, and distract Amir when he's in one of his hyper moods. I even help Dada Jee with his lemon trees.

"Imaan the Responsible," I repeat to myself. It's not too bad. I could get used to it.

I go back to smiling. Lying on this picnic table between my two friends, planning out the summer, feels so good.

"I can't wait to take care of another dog," I say dreamily. "Maybe we'll get a Chihuahua this time. They're so cute!"

"Or one of those mini dogs you can take around in your giant designer purse!" London says with a snort.

Olivia shakes her head. "We already had a dog. I hope we get a different animal this time."

"Like what?" I ask. "A rooster? A piglet?"

"Ooooh, maybe a snake!"

I shiver in pretend disgust. No way am I pet sitting a snake. Then Olivia says, "Pigeons!" and London shudders like there's one right next to her. She's not a big fan of birds. We come up with more weird pets, laughing at one another's guesses.

Finally, London sits up with a little frown. "How will all these pet owners even know about us?" she demands. "We need to go put up those flyers we brought."

She's right, of course. We found our first client, Sir Teddy, because he lives right next door to us. Mrs. Jarrett had to go to the hospital for an emergency and left us in charge of Sir Teddy. I like to think of it as fate. Kismet. Meant to happen.

I also know we can't rely on things like that happening all the time. If we want to have more pet-sitting clients in the future, we need to let people know we exist.

Olivia sits up too. "Good idea. My back is stiff."

We climb down from the picnic table. Olivia picks up her camera and starts taking pictures of the trees in the park. She's always doing that, aiming at something very ordinary and taking dozens of pictures with a *click-click-click*. The pictures always turn out ah-mazing!

I lean into her to look at the camera's display window. "Oh, that came out really nice," I tell her. It's a picture of a squirrel on a low branch, eating an acorn. The squirrel's eyes are huge and gleaming, and it looks close enough to touch.

"Thanks." Olivia shrugs and quickly puts away her camera. She's not convinced of her talent yet.

I roll my eyes at her and grab my backpack. It's filled with flyers we, and Amir, made several days ago. We walk over to the big community bulletin board at the park entrance, and I find an empty space to tack on a couple of flyers. *Must Love Pets. Best Pet Sitters in the Neighborhood! We'll Care for Your Pets Like Our Own. Call Us Today.*

The number on the bottom is my home phone number.

"I hope I get lots of calls," I say. Our home phone hardly ever rings unless it's a telemarketer selling Florida vacations or a new credit card. But now that we're giving out my number for the business, I'm hoping it rings nonstop, making Dada Jee scowl at it.

"I hope we get one call at a time," Olivia replies. "Pets are a handful, you know." She's our pet expert, since she's always pet sitting her aunt's dog.

London stands nearby, handing out flyers to adults who're walking around the park with their kids. "We're very affordable," she tells a lady with a baby stroller. "And we have great references from Mrs. Jarrett, who lives down the street."

The lady smiles and takes a flyer. "What a wonderful idea for a summer project, girls!" she says. "I don't have a pet, but I'll pass this on to my friends."

"It's a real business, not a summer project!" London calls after her, but she hurries away with a wave.

As we leave the park, I remember what London had said a few minutes ago. "Affordable." I repeat the word a few times, liking the way it sits on my tongue.

London turns to me. "Yeah, so?"

"I guess we still need to work out some things for Must Love Pets," I reply. "Like how much we'll charge our customers. And how we'll divide the money we make."

Olivia snaps her fingers. "Oh, we also need to get a written testimonial from Mrs. Jarrett. Something about how great we were with Sir Teddy."

I know what that means. I head toward my house, also known as Must Love Pets headquarters. "We need another team meeting, pronto!"

CHAPTER 2

When we reach my house, it seems empty. Not for long, though. We've just collapsed on the living room couch when I hear the garage door open with a mighty groan. The next minute, Mama and Amir enter the house. Well, Mama enters like a normal person. Amir rushes inside like a hurricane with a mop of black hair and bright eyes.

"We went to the doctor!" Amir shouts. "He stuck a thousand needles in me!"

I raise my eyebrows. "Really? A thousand?"

He nods proudly. "Yes, I counted."

Since he's only six years old, I doubt he can count that high. I ruffle his hair as we all go into the kitchen. "Whoa!" I say, spying the big buckets of lemons lined up on the floor. Dada Jee grows lemon trees in our backyard and is a little bit obsessed with them. Still, he usually stores them on the patio outside.

"Are those . . ." Olivia begins, her eyes round.

"Don't ask." Mama glares at the buckets.

I sigh impatiently. We have more important things to worry about than Dada Jee's gardening habits. "What happened at the allergist?" I ask Mama.

Amir had sneezed nonstop the whole time Sir Teddy was with us, and Mama thought he was allergic to dogs. If that's true, it means really bad news for my pet-ownership dreams. I cross my fingers tightly behind my back and wait for Mama to tell us what the doctor said.

Mama gives the lemons a last glare, then turns

away. "What should we have for lunch, girls?" she asks, opening the fridge door. "I can make pasta if you're all staying."

"Mama!" I say loudly. "What happened at the allergist?"

"Yeah, Mrs. Bashir," London adds, giving me a warning look. "We're all dying to know if Amir got a thousand needles or not."

"I did!" Amir protests, looking offended.

"Well, then, did you cry like a big baby?" I tease.

That annoys him in a major way. "Mama!"

"Imaan, don't be mean to your brother," Mama's voice floats out from the fridge.

"I'm just stating facts," I protest. "He always cries when he gets his shots."

Olivia gives Amir a hug. "They're just being silly, cutie pie," she tells him. "I'm sure you were really brave!"

Mama finally comes out from the fridge. She's got a jar of Alfredo sauce and a packet of shredded cheese in her arms. "He *was* very brave!" she tells us. "The doctor did a skin test. They just scraped the surface of his back a tiny bit."

"And?" I prompt. I'm practically jumping up and down with the need to know. Why can't she just tell us?

Mama gives me a disapproving look. "It was inconclusive."

"Inconclusive?" I repeat. What does that mean?

"That means they're not sure," London adds helpfully.

"Thank you, London." Mama smiles slightly. "The skin test came back negative," she continues. "Which means no allergy."

My heart jumps in my chest. I want to shout with joy, but I make do with a gigantic grin. This is awesome news! Amir isn't allergic to dogs. That means one day—maybe—I can get a dog of my own. Of course, I still have to convince Mama and Dada Jee, but at least they have one less reason to say no.

London and Olivia are also grinning. We give one another little high fives behind our backs.

Wait, Mama looks stern, though. “Why aren’t you happy?” I ask suspiciously.

She puts the sauce and cheese on the counter and leans forward with her elbows. “Since Amir was sneezing so badly, the doctor thinks maybe he’s really allergic in some way. If not to the dog, then to something on the dog, like pollen or dust.”

Olivia frowns. “So how will you know?” she asks. “It could be anything in the world.”

Mama nods. “You’re right. I suppose we just wait and see if it happens again.”

Our grins fade. I want to stomp my foot. This is *so* not helpful. I wish I could find out right away.

Not knowing is way worse than knowing something bad.

Amir pulls at my arm. "Want to see where I got the thousand needles?"

"Uh, no, thanks," I reply. But I give him a quick hug. "Good job on being brave, buddy."

Amir hugs me back, then runs out of the kitchen, shouting, "Hey, Dada Jee! You know how many needles I got today?"

"Tell your grandfather to move these lemons out of my kitchen!" Mama calls after him.

Olivia giggles. Mama sighs and straightens up from the counter. "Lunch, everyone?" she asks, waving the Alfredo jar in front of us.

London nods quickly. "That's good, Mrs. Bashir. We all love pasta."

I'm not sure that's true, since we haven't known Olivia long enough to know her list of favorite foods.

But she gives a thumbs-up and a big smile, which makes Mama smile a little too. "Pasta it is, then," she says. "Come down in thirty minutes, please!"

"Do you need help?" I ask, remembering how I'm supposed to be Responsible Imaan.

Mama literally pushes us out of the kitchen, saying, "I just need some quiet time."

We head to my bedroom and settle on the shaggy rug on the floor. I'm still thinking about what Mama said. "Ugh, allergies suck." I sigh. "Especially if you don't even know what's causing them."

London taps a finger on her chin. "We can use Must Love Pets to check different allergies. Whenever we get a new pet, we'll just note if Amir's sneezing or not. We can even compare which animal makes him sneeze more or less." She snaps her fingers. "We'll make a report."

London is a big fan of reports. She watches a lot

of *Shark Tank* and she's already half a businessperson at age ten.

"Good idea," I reply. If anyone can get to the bottom of Amir's mysterious sneezing, it's London.

I reach into my desk and grab some paper and pens. In a few minutes, we're deep in planning. And giggling. And talking.

I start to get that happy feeling in my chest again. No matter what anyone says, I'm taking Amir's negative allergy test as a win. At least he wasn't sneezing because of me and my pet dreams.

Yup, this summer is definitely going to be awesome.

We're eating a delicious Alfredo pasta lunch when the phone rings. Not Mama's cell phone, but the landline in the hallway that nobody ever uses.

We all freeze and look at one another. "Just ignore it," Dada Jee growls. "Nobody interesting calls on that phone."

London stands up. "That's our business line," she says.

I grit my teeth. It's not like Must Love Pets is a secret, but Mama and Dada Jee both get identical annoyed looks whenever we mention it, so I try not to.

"Business line?" Mama echoes faintly.

"We gave that number to a few people," I reply vaguely, thinking of all the flyers we'd made last week.

"Then you better answer the phone before we all lose our hearing," Dada Jee grumbles, going back to his pasta. He's put red pepper flakes on it and lots of garlic powder. Yuck.

Olivia kicks me on the shin. I move so fast, my chair almost falls over. I jump over a bucket of lemons and charge to the phone, turning slightly as I pick up the receiver. London and Olivia crowd right behind me, eyes wide open. Mama and Dada Jee peek from the doorway. Amir is the only one still sitting at the kitchen table, eating his pasta.

"H-hello?" I whisper. I'm 99 percent sure it's someone selling car insurance. Or maybe a wrong number. I tell myself not to get my hopes up.

London elbows me. "Louder," she whispers. "Customer service, remember?"

I clear my throat and stand up straighter. "Hello?" I say brightly. "This is Must Love Pets. How can I help you?"

Over the phone, I hear a loud crash, followed by meowing. Then a man's voice in my ear growls, "Come down from there!"

CHAPTER 3

Mama is staring at me like she's never seen me before.

Dada Jee's leaning on his cane, eyebrows bunched over his eyes like he's trying to understand what's going on.

Olivia and London are on either side of me. They're literally leaning forward until their ears touch the phone.

I push them a little, and they get the message. "Sorry," Olivia whispers.

The man comes back to the phone. He sounds young and stressed out. "Sorry about that," he says.

"My name's Carl. I'm calling about your pet-sitting service."

I swallow. I know nothing about answering business calls. This is too weird. Then I remember how Mama talks on the phone when she's in her home office. "Yes, how are you?" I ask. "My name's Imaan and I'm in customer service."

Next to me, Olivia giggles a little under her breath.

"I'm fine," Carl says. He takes a deep breath, then lets it out in a whoosh. "Well, actually, I'm not fine, because I have to travel unexpectedly for work. It's last-minute, and I have a plane to catch tomorrow."

He sounds really worried. "Let me guess," I say. "You have a cat that needs taking care of while you're gone?" *We can do this*, I remind myself. *This is easy.*

Carl coughs. "Not one cat," he says. "Three."

"Three?" I squeak. The sounds I'd heard on the phone make more sense now.

Mama's eyes grow big, and she starts to shake her head frantically.

I turn away from her. I know what she's thinking. We had enough trouble with a single dog last week. There's no way we can take care of three pets. Her panic couldn't be more obvious if it were a neon sign over her head.

Carl continues. "Yes, three kittens. They're eight weeks old, and I'm fostering them. Please, can you help? My mom's friend Cora Jarrett told my mom you girls took great care of her dog."

"Oh, that's nice of her." I'm still thinking. Eight-week-old kittens don't sound too bad.

"Kittens are *so* fun," he says. "Cute and cuddly and really no trouble at all. You'll have fun, I promise."

I chew my lip. Three kittens shouldn't be a big

problem since there are three of us: London, Olivia, and me. We could each take care of one, right? Then Carl says, "Just one thing: They're very young, so they need to stay together."

Oh.

I look around. Olivia and London have excited looks on their faces, but Mama and Dada Jee are looking serious, like this is a big deal. Everyone is waiting for me to say something. I take a deep breath, and exhale. Customer service means making the client happy. "Of course. That's what we're here for, Carl. You can travel with zero worries. We're the best pet sitters in the area!"

London mouths *email*, and I remember what we talked about earlier in our team meeting. "If you give me your email address, I'll send you all the details about our fees. Oh, and you need to fill out an intake form too!"

"Oh, thank you so much!" Carl sighs in relief, then starts to rattle off an email address. I grab a pen from the table and start writing on the palm of my hand.

When the call is over, I flick my hair back and stride to the kitchen. I'm feeling on top of the world right now, answering business calls like a professional. Don't mind me if I start dancing or something!

"Well?" London demands from right behind me.

"Three animals, Imaan? What are you thinking?" That's Mama, of course, sinking down on her chair at the kitchen table. "And what's this about fees? I didn't realize you were charging people."

Dada Jee puts a gentle hand on her shoulder. "Let the girl explain."

Mama looks up at him, and I'm shocked to see her face angry. She's never been angry at Dada Jee before. "She'd better explain quickly."

I jump in before there's a war between my mother

and grandfather. "We didn't charge Mrs. Jarett for keeping Sir Teddy because that was our neighborly duty."

Mama's face loses some of its anger. "And now?"

"It's just a small fee, nothing major," London assures her. "We want to look professional, you know. Just like babysitting."

"Kids have a fee for everything nowadays," grumbles Dada Jee.

Mama nods like the matter is settled. "Okay, that makes sense. I guess I'm fine with the fees. But three animals, girls? That's too much!"

I can tell she's coming around. I give her my best smile, pure Imaan the Responsible. "It's not really three separate animals, Mama! It's three itty-bitty adorable kittens, and they need to stay together because they're family."

Actually, I have no idea if they're related. I just

say that because the word *family* means a lot to Mama and Dada Jee.

Oliva and London make identical *aww* faces, with hands clasped under their chins. Amir stares at them, a gooey mess of pasta in his open mouth. Ew.

"Gah-guh!" he says. I think he means "kittens."

Mama relaxes a bit. "That doesn't sound too bad," she admits.

"Carl promised we'd have lots of fun," I say. "He's Mrs. Jarrett's friend's son. She recommended us."

Dada Jee frowns a little. "People shouldn't make promises," he says gruffly. "You can never be certain about the future."

I know why he's saying this. He's thinking of Baba, and how the future changed so drastically when my dad died of cancer four years ago. Dada Jee almost never talks about Baba. When he does, though, there's a sad, faraway look on his face. I slip an arm around his waist for a sideways hug. "I know, Dada Jee," I tell him. "But kittens are always fun, right? They're so cute and mischievous!"

He smiles down at me. "Did I ever tell you about the cat that used to live in our house in Pakistan?" he asks. "She was always having kittens and hiding them around the house. Sometimes under my bed. Sometimes in the back of my closet. I loved all the little ones!"

Surprise kitten presents. That sounds pretty amazing. "You can help us with these kittens, then!" I say cheerfully.

Dada Jee shakes his head, but at least he's not sad anymore. "I have a lot of work this week," he says.

"Let me guess, it's something to do with lemons," I tease, waving my arm at the buckets on the floor.

Dada Jee nods sheepishly.

Mama scowls at him. "Those buckets . . ." she begins.

"I wanna play with kittens too!" Amir shouts, and we all turn to him. His mouth is empty now, but I can see specks of Alfredo sauce on his lips.

I lean over and wipe his mouth with a napkin. "Of course. You can be my helper."

"Are you sure?" Mama taps a finger on the table. "What if Amir starts sneezing again?"

"We have an idea for that, Mrs. Bashir," London jumps in. "We're going to make an allergy report for Amir."

"A what?"

I try not to laugh at Mama's expression. I know London's been waiting for a chance to showcase her *Shark Tank* skills.

I let them talk, and head back upstairs to my room. I have an email to send to Carl, our first official, paying client. I can't wait until we get those cutie kittens in our house!

CHAPTER 4

London and Olivia leave after lunch, but they promise to come back first thing tomorrow morning to welcome Carl and the kittens.

Tomorrow morning is too far away, though. I can't wait to hold those three bundles of joy in my arms. Carl emailed us a picture of them, and they are ADORABLE. One black, one white, and the third's a mixture of colors, like the softest rug.

To stop thinking about the kittens, I pick up my all-time favorite book, *A Wrinkle in Time*. I'm on the eleventh reading, but it still gives me a warm feeling, like a hug. I lie back on my bed, my head on the pillow, reading sideways like I always do.

This book makes me think of Baba, obviously. Meg Murry's dad disappears mysteriously, and she travels all over the universe to find him. How brave is that? Slightly unrealistic, but that's okay. My baba's gone forever, and there's no hope of bringing him back. But I like to remember him—his smiling eyes and his warm laugh. How he took me to the swings in the park and read me bedtime stories. His memory hurts, but I never want to forget him.

Before I know it, I get drowsy. I wake up with a start when I hear Mama yelling. I'm guessing Amir is the culprit. I leap out of bed and head downstairs. Maybe I'll play something with my brother to keep him occupied. Mama is an accountant who works from home, and she can't concentrate if Amir keeps bugging her.

When I get to the kitchen, it's empty except for Dada Jee. He's bent almost to the floor near the pantry. "Where's Amir?" I ask.

"Watching cartoons upstairs," Dada Jee grunts.

"Oh," I say. "Why was Mama making all that racket, then?"

Dada Jee looks up. "That boy isn't the only one your mother gets angry at."

It takes me a few seconds to understand what he means. "She's mad at you?"

He nods like he can't believe it either. I remember Mama's angry face at lunch, after Carl called. Poor Dada Jee. Mama's face can be very scary.

"What are you doing?" I squint at Dada Jee. He's pulling a bucket of lemons across the floor toward the living room. "Wait, let me help," I almost shout. I don't want him falling and hurting himself.

He looks back at me. "Your mother wants me to move these from the kitchen," he grumbles.

I want to ask why Mama was yelling because she never, ever yells at Dada Jee. Something about respect for elders. Then I forget to ask because he's bent over the bucket and straining until his back tenses like a board.

I shoo him out of the way and pull the bucket to his armchair in front of the TV. It's not too heavy, but I stagger just a little. "Here?" I ask.

"Sure, although she won't like that either," Dada Jee says darkly.

I look back at the kitchen floor. "What are you even doing with all these lemons?" I ask. Dada Jee usually harvests a bucket at a time and gifts them to neighbors and friends. My favorite neighborhood café, Tasty, always takes a batch to make smoothies. But right now, there must be hundreds of lemons filling the blue buckets that line the kitchen like soldiers.

He points to them with his cane and pushes me forward. “Don’t stop!”

I groan and push another bucket. Then a third and a fourth. When I’m finished, my back is aching from being bent over, and my forehead is covered with sweat. “This better be for a good reason,” I grumble.

Dada Jee sits in his armchair and studies the lemons like they’ve got the answer to some deep mystery. “I’m going to sell these at the farmers’ market on Thursday.”

I stare at him. He’s never sold his lemons before, as far as I know. Not even Angie, the owner of Tasty, can force him to take money for the lemons he gives her. Mostly, she ends up making free smoothies for him as payment, or sending him home with a big box of delicious baked goods. “But this is your hobby,” I say, confused. "You do it because you enjoy it. Right?"

He doesn't look up. He's poking his cane at the buckets, lining them in a perfectly straight line. "That's exactly what your mother says."

"What do you say?"

Dada Jee shrugs. "I just want to try it out. Mr. Bajpai's wife sells her mint chutney in the farmers' market every week, and it's a huge success. He's always talking about it. I thought, why not try it? It's not going to hurt. Plus, I have too many lemons this year. No one drinks that much lemonade."

Wait a minute, I love Dada Jee's lemonade. I could drink it all day long. He puts a pinch of salt in it along with the sugar, and it tastes out of this world. But I guess he's right—how much lemonade can one family drink?

I have an idea. "Will you sell lemonade too?"

He looks up, surprised. "I don't know. Maybe. I'm

going to check out the market this week, see what sells." Then he frowns. "But your mother thinks it's a bad idea."

I frown too. "Why?"

"I don't know."

I kiss the top of his white hair. "Well, doesn't matter because I think it's a great idea."

He finally smiles. "You do? Maybe I can make it a business like your pet company. What's it called? Loving Pets?"

"Ha! Must Love Pets, Dada Jee!" I squeal, peering at his face to check if he's kidding. His smile is innocent, but then he winks, so I'm not sure. "It's a great idea, though, to start a lemon business."

"Oh yes?"

"Absolutely! You could call it Citrus Delight. Or Love Those Lemons."

He gives me a look. "Those sound dreadful."

"They do not! If you're going to be a professional, you need to think of stuff like names and prices. Just like we did for our pet-sitting business."

He scoffs. "I'm not going to be a professional like you girls. I'm perfectly happy being a gardener. I just want to see if someone will buy these. Baby steps, you know."

Professionals like us. I like the sound of that. I clap my hands, I can't help it. Now that he's got me started, I have tons of ideas. Everyone loves Dada Jee's lemons, so the possibilities are endless. "You could branch out into lemon meringue pie. And lemon cake. Haven't you heard of *go big or go home*, Dada Jee?"

His smile is back. "Another one of your silly American sayings, no doubt."

"Ha!" I reply. Then I have the best idea. "You should ask London to make a business plan for you. She's a genius."

I expect him to shake his head like I'm being too silly. But Dada Jee just goes back to studying his lemons. His cane makes small circles on the living room floor. "Maybe I will," he says quietly, still smiling just a little.

CHAPTER 5

Carl rings the doorbell promptly at nine o'clock in the morning. London, Olivia, and I are waiting near the front door. We're dressed neatly in jeans and T-shirts. London has her signature suit jacket thrown on top like she's a stylish businessperson. "Remind me to order Must Love Pets T-shirts online now that we're getting paid," she whispers just as I reach to open the front door.

I turn to look at her with round eyes. Must Love Pets T-shirts? OMG, I love that idea!

"Open the door!" Olivia whispers from the other side of me.

Mama stands behind us, arms crossed over her chest, mouth unsmiling. Has she never heard of customer service? I smooth my hair and open the door. "Welcome!"

A young giant stands on the front porch, so tall his head almost touches the roof. He's blond, with big beefy hands holding a metal cat carrier and a green scratching post shaped like a cactus. "Hi, I'm Carl," he says shyly.

I decide I like him. "Hi, Carl," I say, smiling warmly. "My name's Imaan."

"Olivia."

"London."

I wait for Mama to say something, but she's quiet. I guess she doesn't need to introduce herself to Carl, since she's not officially part of Must Love Pets.

"Thanks for trusting us with your kittens," I continue, eyeing the cat carrier. I can't really see what's inside, but it sways gently as Carl holds it. I'm guessing there are three little bundles of cuteness overload in there.

Carl grins and hands the carrier to me. "I should be the one thanking you all," he says. "You've really helped me out of a difficult situation. I'm so glad I found you."

"That's what we're here for," London replies cheerfully. "Helping our clients in their time of need." I nod because this is 100 percent true.

She reaches over and takes the scratching post. Carl says, "Let me get the rest from the car."

We all watch as he lumbers down the driveway to his car. How much stuff can kittens need?

I'm so curious about our new clients. I bring the carrier near my face and peer inside. A pair of green eyes stares back, then a little white paw extends out between the bars of the metal door, like a secret handshake. The three of us say "aww" as we watch the paw hover in the air.

I hear the car door slam and look up. The next minute, Carl is back with a backpack in one hand and a round plastic contraption in the other. "There's toys in here and their food," he says, setting the backpack down.

"What's that?" Olivia asks, pointing to the contraption.

Carl grins proudly. "This here is the newest litter box design."

I wrinkle my nose. I'm not a fan of animals pooping, but I guess it goes with the job description.

Olivia nudges me. "At least we won't have to pick up their poop with plastic baggies, like we did with Sir Teddy."

I think of Sir Teddy's walks in the neighborhood, and how we had to clean up after him. Gross.

"Oh no," Carl says, looking very proud. "The kittens are already trained, so they'll use the litter box for all their bathroom needs."

"That's good," Mama says. Finally.

Carl tips his head at her. "Thanks for letting the girls do this, ma'am. I truly appreciate it. I'll be back on Friday afternoon, straight from the airport."

Today's Wednesday, so that means we have almost three full days with the kittens. "They'll be fine," Mama assures him stiffly. "Have a safe trip."

Carl gives us a wave and leaves the porch. He's almost to his car when London calls out, "What are their names?"

He turns with another grin. "The white one's Bella. The black one's Missy. And the mixture is Clyde."

* * *

We stare in fascination at Bella, Missy, and Clyde. They're scampering around my living room, mewling, sniffing at the furniture. "I just want to hug them," Olivia says.

"So hug them," London replies. "But be careful. They may scratch." London's cat, Boots, is old and cranky, and she scratches everyone who comes near.

Olivia carefully picks up the closest kitten—Missy—gently placing one hand on the kitten's chest and using the other hand to scoop up her back paws. "This is how you pick up a cat," she tells us. "I watched a video last night."

Olivia brings Missy in close to her body. I can hear Missy start to purr. It's like being held has put her in a trance. "She likes that," I murmur, surprised.

"That's how we used to pick up our kittens," Dada Jee offers from his armchair. "I remember from my childhood."

"What else do you remember, Dada Jee?" London asks. I love how she calls him that, just like he's her real grandfather. His eyes always crinkle at the corners when she says it, so I'm pretty sure he loves it too.

Dada Jee starts to tell a story about a kitten stuck on the roof of their house in Pakistan. Olivia and London sprawl on the carpet at his feet, Missy in the middle. I half listen as I set up the kittens' things on the far side of the living room near the windows. I can see the backyard and Dada Jee's lemon trees from here. Plus Mama, who's set up her office on the patio today. She's sitting on a lounge chair, laptop on her knees. She'd gone back outside after Carl left, with a warning glance at me. "Don't let those kittens run around the house, Imaan," she'd said.

I'd grumbled a little under my breath at how she focused on me, instead of my friends. It's like she's holding me personally responsible for everything that can possibly go wrong. I guess it makes sense because I'm her daughter. I gave her a salute with my right hand. "Aye, aye, captain."

She didn't think that was funny.

This means I'm watching the kittens very carefully as we sit in the living room listening to Dada Jee's story. "How did you get the cat to come down from the roof?" London asks Dada Jee when he stops to take a breath. Bella, the white kitten, is climbing on her leg.

"I'm coming to that," he replies. "You kids don't have any patience."

Olivia and London giggle, and he goes back to the story with that faraway look he gets every time he talks about things that don't exist anymore. But he's not sad. He's got a glint in his eye like he's enjoying the storytelling even more than my friends are.

A soft scratch on my heel makes me jump. It's Clyde, trying to eat me. "Silly!" I gather him into my arms, rubbing my cheek against his soft fur. He mews and wiggles. I laugh and set him down on the carpet, and he scampers away.

"Here, kitty!" comes a shout from the doorway.

Amir is here. And he's excited. He kneels and picks Clyde up like a bag of potatoes.

"Careful, Amir!" I yelp. "You have to be gentle!"

"I am so gentle!" Amir shouts.

Clyde doesn't look like he agrees. He arches his back and swipes his paws in the air, trying to catch my brother on the nose. Or the eyes. Anywhere will do. "Ow!" Amir shouts again. "Why is he fighting me? I want to be his best friend!"

Olivia rushes over. "That's not how you pick up a cat, silly." She takes Clyde from Amir and drops him on the floor. Clyde shakes himself and runs off to join his sisters, who are playing with Dada Jee's sock-covered feet.

Amir's lip trembles, and his face gets red. "But I want to hold him!" he wails at the top of his lungs.

Great. It took all of twenty minutes to start a pet disaster.

CHAPTER 6

I'm not sure what to do. I can see Mama outside talking on the phone. If she's on a call with a client and there's noise in the background, she gets really upset. She says it makes her seem unprofessional.

Now that I have Must Love Pets, I understand what she means. Amir's yelling makes me want to hide my animal clients from him until he calms down. "Amir, stop!" I say firmly.

"You stop!" he screams.

I exchange looks with Dada Jee. He shakes his head and starts getting up. He's Amir's caretaker while Mama's working, and he knows how to deal with tantrums. "How about we get a cookie, huh, buddy?"

I roll my eyes. Bribing a kid with cookies when he's already hyper. Does Dada Jee think that will really work?

"No!" Amir says loudly, stomping his foot. "No cookie!"

Dada Jee sighs. "They're your favorite, chocolate chip." He's already walking toward the kitchen, leaning on his cane.

Amir looks longingly in Dada Jee's direction but doesn't budge. I can't help but admire him. This kid knows what he wants. "Kitty!" he repeats stubbornly. "Now!"

I sigh. I'd do anything for a chocolate chip cookie right now.

"Wait!" Olivia puts up a hand. "We're not

stopping you from playing with the kittens, Amir. We just want to make sure you don't hurt each other."

Amir rubs a finger over his face. "He didn't hurt me," he mumbles. But I can see a faint red line on his cheek.

I melt a little. I didn't realize Clyde had scratched Amir. Maybe that's why my brother's upset. He doesn't handle pain very well.

Olivia puts her arm around his shoulder. "I know, buddy. But I want you to learn the right way to pick the kittens up. Then we'll let you play with them, okay?"

"How?" Amir asks, frowning.

She pulls him toward the stairs. "Let's watch some videos in Imaan's room."

"And put some ointment on his cheek too, please!" I call out after them.

Olivia waves to let me know she heard me. I sigh in relief as the two disappear upstairs together. Dada Jee comes back from the kitchen and sits down in his armchair again. "I'm too old for this," he mumbles, and closes his eyes.

Crisis averted, for now.

"EEEK!" London squeals.

Maybe not.

"What happened?" I ask, looking around wildly. My heart beats so fast, my chest feels tight. Unlike Amir, London never yells. "What happened, London?" I ask again.

She's looking horrified. She points to the curtains on the windows overlooking the backyard. They're heavy and gray, and one of them is swinging wildly as a kitten climbs up. Using claws and teeth. And tail.

Missy.

I clap a hand over my mouth. "We have to get her down," I whisper. "Now!"

Dada Jee opens his eyes and nods wisely. "Yup, they're sly fellows, these kittens. You can't leave them alone for a minute."

"Dada Jee! You're not helping!" I moan.

He waves to the laundry room off the kitchen. "There's a stepladder in there."

I rush to grab the little ladder and set it against the wall near the curtain. I can see Mama from where I'm standing. She's still on the phone, but she's now pacing up and down the yard near the trees. Good. That means she probably can't tell what's happening inside.

I look back at the curtain. Missy is halfway up now. If she gets to the top, I won't be able to reach her. I climb up the ladder and extend my hand.

Missy stops and stares at me. "Come here, girl," I croon.

She blinks. Then she climbs one more step.

London taps my leg. "Here, give her this." I look down. It's a pink toy mouse.

Really? Kittens are pretty smart. I'm sure they know mice aren't pink. Not the ones you can eat anyway. Still, I take the toy and shake it near Missy's head. "Here, want to play?"

Missy stares at the mouse. I guess it means she's thinking about it. "I know it's not a real mouse, Missy, but it's better than the curtain," I say. "You don't want my mama to see you. There will be consequences, you know."

Missy blinks some more. Then she yawns.

I shake the mouse, and very unexpectedly she jumps at it. I lose my balance as she lands on my shoulder. "London, help!" I shout.

London grabs my leg to steady me, but that just makes me wobble even more. *Don't grab the curtain, don't grab the curtain*, I tell myself like a mantra. If the curtain falls, there's no way we can hang it up by ourselves again. The top of the window reaches way past my head.

I'm still wobbling as I try to think. Thinking is impossible, though. Everything is too loud. Dada Jee is standing up, waving his arms around, shouting, "Settle down, child!" London is holding on to my leg and saying, "Stop shaking, Imaan!" over and over. I can hear music from my laptop upstairs and Amir laughing loudly.

It's no use. I fall.

The good news: I'm not gripping the curtain, so it stays put. The bad news: The stepladder is about four feet high, so the floor feels as hard as rock when I reach it.

"Ow!" I whisper.

"Are you okay?" London asks, horrified.

I lie on the floor with my eyes closed, kitten toys scattered around me. "I'm fine."

Dada Jee grunts from his spot near the armchair. "Really, Imaan, you should be more careful."

I grit my teeth. "You're right."

Then my eyes fly open because I hear mewling from the far side of the room. It's almost an echo, which means A KITTEN HAS GONE WANDERING.

This is literally what Mama warned me about. She's going to hold me personally responsible for anything that happens. I jump up and look around wildly. "Where's that sound coming from?"

London is staring at the archway that leads into the kitchen. "There," she says, pointing.

I gulp at the sight. Bella, Missy, and Clyde are all sauntering across the kitchen table, their tails up in the air like they're really proud of themselves. The worst part: They're stepping all over food—a stick of butter, a few leftover pancakes from breakfast. Bella licks the butter like it's her best friend. Clyde sticks his face into a glass half full of water and manages to spill it very quickly. Missy, of course, wants to climb again. She has jumped from the table onto the counter, where she gets her paws on the side of a big bag of sugar and leaps.

"Noooooo!" I leap as well, over the kitten toys and across the living room. I'm going so fast that my feet slide against the tiles and I almost lose my balance. London is right behind me.

Too late. The bag of sugar teeters under Missy, and then falls. She yowls and falls to the ground, sugar showering around her like white rain.

London and I are breathing harshly as we reach the mess on the counter. I gasp. "Oh God, Mama will have a fit."

Missy scampers over to the edge of the counter

and mews hello. I just stare at her, trying to control my breathing. Trying not to think of what Mama will do if she walks in right now.

Dada Jee comes and stands next to us, hands on his hips. "The cats in Pakistan never did anything like this," he says in a very disapproving tone.

CHAPTER 7

"We have to clean up," I tell London. Actually, I plead. I'm not sure how this mess can be cleaned up.

She looks at me like I'm being very foolish. "There's no time! We have to catch the kittens first."

She's right. If we don't get the kittens back in the living room, they'll just make a mess somewhere else.

"How about you catch the kittens, I'll clean?" I suggest.

"Alone? I need at least one more person!"

I scowl at her. Why is she always so reasonable?

"You don't know Mama. Keeping the house clean is my responsibility. If she sees this . . ."

London looks outside through the kitchen window. "Where is she anyway? I thought she was working outside."

"She went out through the backyard gate," Dada Jee says helpfully. "I think she was talking to one of the neighbors."

That means we have no time to lose. I spring into action, scooping Missy in my arms. "Come on, you troublemaker!" I say, panting.

Missy meows in protest. I totally ignore her and stomp back into the living room. "Get the other two!" I yell to London.

"I can't find them!" London yells back.

I look around for a safe place to put Missy. I need a fence or something. A kitty prison. "How does Carl do this?" I mutter.

Missy meows again, louder this time. Her paw waves close to my face, and I dodge. No way am I letting her scratch me. I put her inside her cat carrier and shut the little door. "Stay there!"

"What's going on?" Olivia says from the staircase.

I look up. "No time to lose," I say. "Help London find the other two!"

Amir is right behind Olivia. "I want to play with the kittens," he demands. "I'm a expert now."

I say nothing about his horrible grammar. I wave him over to me and push him down next to the cat carrier. "You can watch Missy, but don't open the door. She's in a time-out."

Amir lies sideways and peers into the carrier with fascinated eyes. "Was she being bad?" he whispers.

I'm already halfway to the kitchen. "Very bad," I reply in a tough voice.

The kitchen is in chaos. Olivia and London are

both on their knees, looking for Bella and Clyde. Dada Jee is trying to sweep the sugar on the ground into the dustpan, but he's also trying to hold on to his cane at the same time, so nothing actually gets done. I take a huge breath to calm myself down. *One thing at a time.*

I start picking up food from the kitchen table. The plates go in the dishwasher, even though they were clean earlier. The butter that Bella licked goes right into the trash can. Gross.

"Gotcha!" Olivia yells. I look up. She's holding Clyde by the scruff of his neck, but he's not calm like in the videos. He's swinging his body in wild arcs like a pendulum. And he's growling. Loudly.

"I think he's mad," I say nervously.

"You think?" Olivia drops Clyde back onto the floor like a hot potato. He lands on his feet and darts under a chair. She drops down too, facedown on the floor. "Where did you go, you adorable monster . . ."

Before anyone can move, the kitchen door swings open, and Mama walks in. She's followed by our neighbor Mr. Greene, a big and stern-looking older man with a mustache, and tattoos on his wrinkled arms. He lives next door to us but hardly ever talks to anyone. The door bangs behind them, and we all jump.

Dada Jee is so startled he drops his cane and sinks against the counter. The dustpan he was holding drops to the floor.

Great. Now the sugar is even more scattered.

"What on earth is going on?" Mama says. She's staring at the sugar all over the kitchen floor.

"Nothing, just a little accident!" I squeak, picking up the broom and sweeping randomly around me. "We'll have it cleaned up in no time."

Olivia nods from her place on the floor.

"Absolutely," she says, smiling brightly. "Everything is fine!"

Bella chooses that moment to run across the room and attack the silver buckles on Mr. Greene's boots. He grunts and shakes his foot. "You have kittens?" he asks in a gruff voice.

"No, no," Mama replies quickly. "My daughter and her friends are taking care of someone's pets for a few days."

London stands up and gives him a little wave. "We're Must Love Pets, a female-owned pet-sitting business. I can get you a business card if you're interested."

My eyes pop. Female-owned? Business cards? What's even going on right now?

Mama sends London a look that's half impressed and half horrified. "He's not interested." Then she takes a deep breath and continues, "Mr. Greene was asking me some accounting questions about his Etsy store, and I offered him some lemonade."

This rough-looking man has an Etsy store? I try not to stare at him. What does he make, swords? I place the broom carefully against the wall and turn to get some of Dada Jee's freshly squeezed lemonade from the fridge.

"Hello," Mr. Greene grunts. Funny, he sounds just like Dada Jee.

"Etsy is a cool website," Olivia says. "What do you make at your store?"

He looks like he's not going to reply. He's too busy moving his boots away from Bella's pouncing paws. Finally he says, "Ah, photos of nature. Things like that."

I put a jug of lemonade on the kitchen table and pour Mr. Greene a glass, hoping he'll forget about Bella. "That sounds nice. Olivia's a photo artist too."

Mr. Greene's face gets red. "I'm not an artist," he mumbles, taking a big gulp of lemonade.

"Mr. Greene is a Vietnam veteran," Mama adds.

I smile. "Just like Dada Jee!" I turn to my grandfather. "Tell Mr. Greene about the war you fought in! There were tanks and everything, right?"

Dada Jee grunts like it's no big deal. "I don't like talking about it."

This is true. He hardly ever talks about the war, or anything sad. I feel bad for bringing it up. I turn back to Mr. Greene. "How do you like the lemonade? It's homemade."

Mr. Greene takes a slower sip. "Mmmm."

Dada Jee nods in approval. "You like it, eh? Straight from my lemon trees in the backyard."

"You made this?" Mr. Greene's eyes widen. "It's really good. You should sell it."

Mama makes a deep noise in her throat. I try

not to laugh. Is this what she'd been fighting with Dada Jee about?

Dada Jee pours himself a glass of lemonade. "That's a good idea," he says slowly. "Maybe you can tell me more about this Etsy someday."

Mama practically pushes Mr. Greene back outside. "It was so nice to talk with you," she tells him. "I'll write up a quote for my accounting services and email you."

He nods at us and leaves. Mama follows him out, turning to glare at me at the last minute. "Clean. Up. This. Mess."

Once she's gone, I get down on my knees to help Olivia search for the missing kittens. London does the same. After a moment, we find them under a chair, licking at sugar. "Naughty babies!" I scold them. Olivia and London each pick up one, and we head to the living room.

“Imaan!” Amir wails as we reach him. “Missy’s gone!”

My heart sinks. The cat carrier is wide open, and Missy is most definitely not inside.

Why did I think pet sitting three kittens would be easy?

CHAPTER 8

Quickly, London, Olivia, and I clean up the kitchen. It doesn't take long, now that the kittens are out of the way.

Well, two of them anyway. Bella and Clyde are imprisoned in the cat carrier, with Amir as their gleeful warden. I shouldn't let him be in charge again, since he somehow let Missy out in the first place. But I don't really have a choice right now. It's all hands on deck because we have a runaway kitten to catch.

I just hope Amir doesn't let the other two escape. Ugh, that would be terrible.

He dangles the pink mouse toy just outside the carrier door. "Come and get it, kitty!" he whispers. "Come and get your mouse!"

The kittens stick their noses out of the holes in the door. Their paws too. Amir thinks this is the funniest thing ever. "You can't get it!" he chortles.

"Stop being mean, Amir," I tell him. I'm lying on the ground, my legs up on the couch. Olivia is in the exact pose next to me, our shoulders touching.

"*You're* being mean," Amir informs me. "You're not letting me play with them."

I close my eyes with a sigh. He's right. The kittens should be scampering about, playing. They're babies; they need their space. But I don't have any way of limiting them, so I've stuck them inside their carrier.

I guess you can call me Mean Imaan.

"You need an enclosure of some kind," Dada Jee

says from his armchair. "Like one of those things human babies play in."

Olivia snaps her fingers. "A playpen! That would be perfect."

I sigh again. "Where can I get a playpen? Nobody we know has kids that age. Plus, right now we have bigger problems."

"What bigger problems?"

I look at her like she's lost her senses. "A kitten on the prowl? Did you forget Missy?"

She waves her hand at London, who's crawling on the floor, looking under the couches. "London's taking care of it."

"Thanks!" comes London's muffled voice.

I'm staring at my left leg, which is touching a cushion on the couch. "Maybe we can make a wall . . ." I say slowly, poking the cushion with my big toe.

"A wall?" Olivia asks. "With what?"

I sit up and grab the cushion. "Amir, I have a job for you!" I call out. I have an idea growing in my head. If we pile things together, the kittens won't be able to wander off. Then we can let them out.

Amir stands up quickly. "Yes, yes! I can do it!"

"You don't even know what it is yet."

He's literally hopping. "I can do anything, I just know it!"

Olivia giggles. I sigh. "Go into all the bedrooms and get every pillow you can find."

Amir looks disappointed. "That's it? That's nothing special."

Olivia sits up too and taps a finger on her watch. "It's special if it's a race, buddy. You have sixty seconds, you better hurry!"

"Ooh, I'm gonna win!" Amir goes to stand at the bottom of the staircase, one hand on the banister. "You gotta say 'ready, steady, go!' "

"See what you started?" I whisper to Olivia.

She shrugs. "What? It's fun!" She takes a deep breath and shouts, "Ready. Steady. Go!"

Amir clatters up the stairs like his pants are on fire. "You can do it, Amir!" London yells after him.

"Your mama won't be pleased," Dada Jee warns.

"About the race or the pillows?"

"Both," he replies. "But mostly the pillows."

He's right, of course. Mama doesn't like cushions and pillows on the floor. Amir's always leaving crumbs of Cheetos and spilling apple juice wherever he goes. Our floors aren't the cleanest.

"I don't have a choice," I say grimly. No matter what I do, Mama will protest. Then I think of the forts I used to build with Baba on this same living room floor, and I cheer up. Maybe Mama will also remember the fun times we used to have when Baba was alive. I smile at Dada Jee. "It'll look great, you'll see."

Olivia and I begin piling up the couch cushions in a line on the floor, like a soft, cushiony fence around the carrier. Amir clatters back down the stairs three times before the sixty seconds run out. His face is red with excitement, arms full of pillows from the bedrooms. "You did great!" Olivia says, tapping her watch again. London and Dada Jee clap for him.

"Told you I was the fastest!" He pants, flopping down on a couch.

I hug his sweaty little body. He's actually been really helpful. The wall is long and colorful, made of cushions, pillows, and even the beanbag from my room. It won't stop the kittens completely, but it will definitely slow them down.

"This looks cool," Amir announces. "Like a castle."

I nod happily. It's true. The kittens have a very nice, soft castle to play in as long as they don't try to knock down the walls and escape again.

I carefully open the door to the cat carrier. For a few seconds nothing stirs, then both Bella and Clyde shoot out at the same time. "Here, Amir," I beckon. "Come sit in the middle."

Amir sits down in the center of the room inside the cushion wall, cat toys all around him. Bella climbs onto his lap, trying to get to the pink mouse. Clyde sniffs his feet, and I secretly wonder how he's surviving the smell. My little brother is not fond of baths.

There's a movement from the corner of the room. "I got her!" London announces triumphantly, holding up a little black ball of fur. Missy yowls to let us know what she thinks. Soon, she's also playing around inside our cushion castle, meowing happily.

Amir, of course, is laughing in delight. "Look at me, Imaan!"

I look. He's got two kittens playing in his lap, plus their toys. A third kitten is trying to climb up his chest. Missy, of course. She obviously loves exploring. Amir looks like a little scarecrow, with his arms stretched out. "Having fun?" I ask, ruffling his hair gently.

He nods, his face shining.

There's peace for exactly seven minutes and thirty-two seconds. I know this because I can see the microwave clock in the kitchen. We're all looking at Amir and his three friends until Mama walks back into the house.

She watches us for a minute, her hands crossed over her chest. "This looks like fun," she finally says.

I eye her carefully. Mama's idea of fun is a long bath with soft music and absolutely no kids allowed. I'm guessing no animals either. "The kittens are adorable, aren't they?" I ask hopefully.

Mama nods. Then she says, "They're going to get sick if they eat lemons."

What's she talking about? I frown and look around. Clyde has reached Dada Jee's feet and is trying to sneak under them to play with the basket of lemons still there from the night before. "Hey, come out from there!" Amir yells, and scoots a little to grab Clyde.

The kittens think it's a game. They crawl under Dada Jee's feet and attack the lemon buckets. A few lemons roll away, and Bella pounces on them.

"Great!" London groans.

Mama's mouth twitches. "I thought the lemons had been removed?" she says to Dada Jee.

Dada Jee harrumphs. "They'll be gone tomorrow," he replies darkly.

Mama's face changes. It's tighter now, like she's drunk a glass of lemonade with zero sugar. "So you're definitely going to the farmers' market tomorrow to sell them?"

He nods.

She nods too.

London, Olivia, and I stare at the two of them. It's like they're mad at each other, but they don't want to talk about it. I remember what Dada Jee said the day before, about Mama not being happy with him selling lemons. I open my mouth to ask why, but Mama turns on her heels. "Pick up those pillows from the floor," she orders.

Then she exits, leaving us all staring after her.

CHAPTER 9

We decide to go to Olivia's house for dinner.

There are many reasons for this:

A. When Sir Teddy was our client, he'd spent all his time at my place, and that made London and Olivia mad. I definitely want to do things differently this time.

B. The kittens need a change of scenery.

C. Mama needs to forget the kittens exist. She found the butter in the trash earlier and almost threw a fit. Something about kids not understanding the value of things.

I told her she didn't want to eat the butter anymore, now that it had Bella's tongue marks all over it.

That made her face very, very red.

Before things could get worse, Olivia called her mom to ask if we could have dinner at their place. Mrs. Gordon didn't mind at all as long as we helped with cleanup afterward.

I secretly wish I *never* have to clean up anything ever again, but that's probably not going to happen. At least I have my friends with me to make the job easier.

We eat chicken quesadillas in Olivia's dining room. It's got a high ceiling and big windows, but it's one of the few rooms that's fully set up. Olivia's family moved to this house a week ago, and there are still boxes everywhere. "You should see the upstairs," Olivia jokes. "It's a mess."

"Kind of like my living room, huh?" I joke back, remembering the cushion wall.

London pats me on the back. "Hey, don't worry. Pet sitting can get messy sometimes."

"Plus that wall idea was genius!" Olivia adds.

I feel a glow in my chest. "That's me, a genius!" I mumble awkwardly.

I jump as sharp claws rake across my foot. "Hey!" I yelp. We've let the kittens roam free on the dining room floor while we eat dinner. The door is closed, and there's not much furniture in the room for them to hide under. "Stop scratching!"

London giggles, then yelps too and shakes her feet so much, the dining table shudders.

Then we all start giggling.

The door opens, and a teenage boy with floppy blond hair strides in, holding a plate of food. It's Olivia's older brother. "Hi, Jake," I say cheerfully. He's one of my favorite people ever, since he helped us organize a search party for Sir Teddy the week before.

"What are you doing here?" Olivia asks, scowling. I guess he's not *her* favorite person.

Funny how brothers and sisters never get along.

Jake closes the door and takes a seat at the table. "I don't want to eat with the parents," he grumbles good-naturedly. "They're boring."

"Well, you can't eat with us," Olivia replies. "This is girls only."

"Clyde isn't a girl," I point out.

Olivia gives me a dirty look, but she doesn't say anything else. "Clyde who?" Jake asks me, taking a bite of quesadilla.

I'm about to reply, but just then he yells, "Ow!" and the three of us start giggling again. "What on earth is that?" he says, jumping up.

"Jake, meet Bella, Missy, and Clyde," Olivia says, trying to keep a straight face. "Our latest clients."

Jake bends under the table and peeks at the kittens.

"At least they're adorable," he says. "Better keep them away from Pixie, though."

"Who's Pixie?" I ask.

Jake emerges from under the table and fixes his hair. "My parakeet."

London and I exchange shocked looks. How did we not know Jake had a parakeet? "Can we see her?" I ask eagerly.

"Really, Imaan?" London says dryly. "Don't we have enough on our plate right now with these three devil kittens?"

"I was just asking."

"Well, don't."

I wink at her. I really can't help teasing her. She's not a fan of birds, especially those that get into her personal space.

Jake sits and starts eating again. "Pixie's already gone to sleep," he tells us. "Maybe next time."

I turn away from London to eye Jake, not sure if he's telling the truth. I have no idea how early parakeets go to bed. "Promise?" I ask.

He shrugs. "Sure. Would I lie to you?"

I'm not sure how to answer that, so I shrug.

Olivia rolls her eyes and stands up. "Come on, forget Pixie. Let's clean up and take the kittens upstairs to my room. Mom found a huge box to use as a playpen."

Olivia's room is mostly empty, but there's a bed with a dresser. We sit on the floor and look at the empty TV box Mrs. Gordon saved for us. It's humongous. "I've never seen a TV that big," London whispers.

"My dad loves watching football on a big screen," Olivia replies.

"Big?" I repeat. "More like giant." I'm totally

envious. Our TV is half this size and older than me. There's a spot in the middle where the pixels have died, and it's impossible to miss.

If Must Love Pets gets famous, I'm getting a giant TV for my room.

We put the kittens inside the box. They start sniffing and crawling around. I open the backpack Carl left with us and take out a few of the small toys. "This should make them happy."

"I think they like human toes more," London says.

Olivia sighs. "How can they be so adorable? I just want to eat them up!"

"Okay, first of all, ew!" London says. "Second of all, all baby animals are adorable by nature. It's basically how they survive. Who's going to hurt a kitty that looks at you with such big, cutie-pie eyes?"

We all think about this for a minute. Then I say, "Your cat, Boots, is the opposite of adorable, though."

London nods slowly. "That's because she's perfectly capable of taking care of herself."

"I think she's a witch in disguise."

"I'm not ruling it out."

We watch the kittens for a while. It sounds boring, but it's totally not. They're so cute and cuddly, with their twitching noses and wide eyes. Bella and Missy both have green eyes, and Clyde's are blue. I'd hug them if they weren't so prickly and bite-y.

Olivia brings out her camera and snaps some pictures. "OMG, look!" She turns the camera to show us the LCD display. The filters on the camera have made the kittens look really amazing.

"You take great pictures," I tell her.

"Anyone can do it," she says, rolling her eyes.

I haven't known Olivia very long, but I'm starting to figure her out. She's super artistic. Creative. But not at all proud of it. It's like she doesn't even know how good she is. I reach over and give her a sideways hug. "You do it better," I say firmly, and she offers a shy smile.

The kittens keep us busy all evening. Mrs. Gordon brings us popcorn later, and we watch a movie on Olivia's laptop. It's almost like a sleepover, only London and I have to go home at the end of it.

When the movie ends, I peek into the TV box. The kittens are fast asleep, curled up against one another likc BFFs.

"Good-bye, babies," I whisper, touching one fingertip to a soft head.

"Are you sure you're okay with leaving them here tonight?" Olivia asks, chewing her lip.

I think back to last week when I'd been upset with my friends for wanting to take Sir Teddy away from me. I give Olivia a big smile. "Positive," I reply.

Missy yawns in her sleep. I yawn too. "See you tomorrow," I tell my friends, both human and animal.

CHAPTER 10

Dada Jee is in a tizzy the next morning. "Hurry, Mr. Bajpai will be here soon with his van!" he growls at me as I eat breakfast.

I look at him with narrowed eyes. "For what?" I ask. "And why do *I* need to hurry?"

"We're going to the farmers' market," he says, like I should already know this. "We need his van to cart all my lemons."

I remember his plans for the buckets of lemons in the living room. I bet Mama will be glad to see them gone. Then I frown. "Why me? I have to take care of the kittens!"

"Everyone's going, even those ridiculous kittens," he replies. "Your mother said she doesn't want the kittens to stay in the house without adult supervision. If I go, you all have to go with me."

"She was pretty mad about the mess yesterday," I agree. Then I think of something. "Can London and Olivia come too?"

Dada Jee shrugs and gestures with both hands toward my breakfast. I guess that means *hurry up*. "Sure, if they want to. They need to check with their parents first."

I gobble up the rest of my toast and gulp down my juice. Then I rush to call London and Olivia and inform them of the change of plans. Both girls were going to spend the day with me anyway, so their parents don't mind. The farmers' market is a well-known place just a twenty-minute walk from our street. If it wasn't for Dada Jee's lemons (or the kittens' carrier), we could easily walk there.

I get dressed in jeans and a T-shirt that says DON'T WORRY, BE HAPPY. Then I find Amir and help him get ready. He has a hundred extremely annoying questions, and he never stops to hear the answers. "Why are we going? What will we do there? Will I meet lots of farmers? Can I buy lots of things? I need new toys. Many, many toys."

I sigh as I push his arms into the sleeves of a clean T-shirt. "It's not a mall. It's an open-air market with fruits and veggies, mostly."

He makes a face. "I don't like veggies."

"Yes, I'm aware."

"You'll have to buy me something else. I won't eat any veggies!"

I can see that he's starting to get upset, so I distract

him by holding his jeans up to his face. “Here, put these on real quick.”

“Can I eat lots of ice cream?” he asks. “And popcorn?”

I kneel to put on his socks. “You’ll have to ask Dada Jee.”

“Dada Jee said he’ll be busy with his lemon stall,” he says, pouting his cute little lips. “He said you’re the boss of me today.”

I tug his unruly hair. “I’m always the boss of you, silly goose!”

“Nah-uh!”

He’s looking so indignant that I reach over and give him a hug. Of course, he wiggles, and then it turns into my signature tickle hug. Which he loves.

Okay, who am I kidding? I may be ten, but I love tickle hugs too. Baba used to give the best ones, and now I’m carrying on the tradition with Amir.

I don't realize I've stopped laughing and tickling until Amir asks, "What's wrong?"

"Nothing," I say. Then I pause. Maybe he won't care if I talk about Baba. Neither Mama nor Dada Jee likes talking about him, which sometimes makes me feel like maybe he didn't even exist. Maybe he was just in my imagination.

Who's being a silly goose now? "Baba used to hug me like this," I say softly.

Amir hides his head in my shoulder. "Oh." Then he says very quietly, "I don't even remember him."

"I do," I reply just as quietly. "I'll tell you about him someday."

"Okay."

We stay like that for a minute. Then Mr. Bajpai honks his horn from the driveway, and we let go of each other. Amir pelts down the stairs, shouting,

"I'll get it!" even though nobody rang the bell, and he's not allowed to open the front door anyway.

I shake my head and follow him.

Outside, a young man is hauling lemon buckets into a huge white van. I think he's Mr. Bajpai's grandson or something. Dada Jee hovers over him with his cane. "Be careful, you!" he growls.

I feel sorry for the young man. "Do you need help?" I ask awkwardly.

"He's got muscles, don't worry." Dada Jee points his cane down the street. "You go get your friends."

Good idea. I settle Amir into the van, clip his seat belt, and say, "Don't move!" Then I head down the street to get my friends. And my furry clients. The kittens are already in their cat carrier, their tiny paws extending out as they test the morning air. "They ate their food and used the litter box with zero problems," Olivia reports proudly.

Ew. I hadn't even thought about the litter box. "Great," I say weakly.

"Let's go!" London says, bouncing on her feet. She's not wearing her suit jacket for once, just capri pants and a T-shirt. A small purse dangles from one shoulder. "I got money to buy us drinks and snacks," she says, patting the purse.

I grin. That's an excellent idea.

Mr. Bajpai honks the horn again, and we run to the van holding hands. Olivia has the cat carrier and London's holding the cat backpack. They get in first, laughing and pushing each other. I go back into the house to let Mama know we're leaving.

She's sitting on the patio again, reading something on her laptop. "Do you need me to do anything for you before I go?" I ask.

She looks up and smiles. "No thanks, *jaan*. Have fun!"

I can't tell if she's truly happy about this farmers' market expedition. She definitely wants all the noise and chaos out of the house so she can work. Still, she wasn't too excited about Dada Jee's plans to sell lemons. "Are you sure . . ." I begin.

She's already back to her laptop. "Take care of your brother, please."

When I go back outside, Mr. Greene, the grumpy neighbor, is standing in his driveway, holding a coffee mug in his hand. "Hi!" I call out, waving.

He glares at me like I've committed the worst offense. His mustache quivers.

"We're going to the farmers' market to sell my granddad's lemons," I add for absolutely no reason.

I think I'm babbling. I blame the mustache.

Mr. Greene stops glaring. "Very good," he says. "That was good lemonade."

I grin. "I'll bring you some more soon," I promise.

That brings back the glare, as if he's totally regretting his decision to talk to me. He takes a sip of his coffee.

I have so many questions. Why is he so grumpy? Did he get injured in the war? Maybe he and Dada Jee could be friends.

Okay, that last one isn't a question, but it's definitely something to think about. This man looks like he needs a friend or two.

Mr. Bajpai honks his horn for the third time. It's so loud it echoes up and down the street. "Bye, see you later!" I yell to Mr. Greene, and rush toward the van.

He just turns away like he didn't hear me.

Yeah, right. He definitely needs a friend.

CHAPTER 11

The farmers' market is the coolest place on earth. Seriously.

It's full of bright colors and amazing smells. Vegetables. Fruits. Flowers. Honey. Pastries. I can even see a Ferris wheel in the distance behind all the tents. There are rides. Amir will absolutely love that.

A man passes by with a cart full of freshly baked bread. Yum. The market isn't even open yet and I'm drooling. "I'm glad I brought money," London mutters.

“I may need to borrow some,” I reply.

We find Dada Jee’s designated table next to a woman selling watermelons, and start setting up. That’s when we face our first problem. Dada Jee’s idea of selling is to dump the lemon buckets on the plastic folding table and sit grumpy-faced on a folding chair nearby. “Easy,” he says, twirling his cane in his hand. “We’ll be done in no time.”

London, Olivia, and I all gape at him. “But . . . but . . .” London sputters.

Even Amir looks shocked, like he can’t believe sales is so easy.

The watermelon lady just chuckles softly. Her table has a checkered tablecloth and hand-written price signs. A few of the watermelons are cut open into fancy star shapes.

London takes a deep breath and starts again. “Let us help you, Dada Jee.”

He glares at her. "I don't need help."

"Yes, you really do," I tell him, hands on hips. "We're professionals, remember?"

He doesn't say anything, so we take charge.

Olivia takes out a pink Must Love Pets flyer from her bag (she brought a whole stack to hand out later). She turns it over to write lemon prices with a black Sharpie. I watch as she makes it all pretty and swirly, then tapes it on the edge of the table.

"Here." The watermelon lady brings out an extra tablecloth and offers it to us. "Make the table look nice."

I want to hug her, but I stop myself because that would be too weird. "Thank you," I say, smiling. "Your watermelons look delicious."

She smiles back like I gave a her a huge compliment. "They most definitely are."

"Do you grow them in your backyard like my grandfather?"

She wrinkles her nose. "Well, it's more like a whole plot of land next to my house. But yes, I do grow them myself."

"Ooh, maybe you can give my grandfather some tips. He's always complaining about pests and things."

Dada Jee clears his throat in warning. I give him a very beautiful smile, like I have no idea what his problem is.

The woman nods. "Anytime." She walks back to her chair and settles down with a book. "You kids come by in the afternoon when it gets hot. I'll share some watermelon with you if I have any leftovers."

We get back to work setting up. I spread the tablecloth, then arrange the lemons in small yellow piles. London and Olivia help me. Soon, all the buckets are empty and Dada Jee's lemon stand looks gorgeous.

"Perfect!" Olivia claps her hands.

Dada Jee grunts, but I can tell he's pleased. Finally, he says very softly, "Thank you, girls."

I look around for Amir. He's sitting on the ground, peering into the cat carrier. I nudge him with my foot. "Now let's take a look around the market!"

We leave the kittens with Dada Jee and stroll around the marketplace. The three of us are arm in arm, and Amir skips along in front of us. Soon, the gates open, and people start streaming in. I breathe in the air. "Hungry?" I ask.

"Yesss!" Amir jumps a little.

"What should we eat first?"

We end up eating everything. Fresh almond croissants. Strawberry chocolate cupcakes. Mini quiches. Some kind of homemade raisin bread that tastes awesome. In less than an hour, we're full and very happy.

"Why don't we come here every week?" London asks. "This is heaven."

"I know, right?" Olivia replies happily.

Then Amir pulls at my hand. "Look, goats!" He starts running like a maniac, me behind him.

Olivia doesn't move. "I'll get the kittens," she calls out. "They shouldn't be stuck in their carrier for so long."

I wave to her as I'm dragged along by my brother. "Meet us near the goats!" I call out.

I'm not exactly sure why there are goats at a farmers' market. Turns out it's a petting zoo. There are not only goats but also some cows and two pigs. They're tucked into the far corner of the market, which is practically empty at this time of the day. "Come in!" A teenage girl with long brown braids opens the fence enclosure for us. "Just a few pennies to brush goat fur."

"Cool!" yells Amir. I let him go. He rushes to the nearest goat with a brush in his little hand and a determined look on his face.

The goats are mostly cute. White, brown, patchwork . . . they all crowd around Amir like he's their hero. One chomps on the end of his T-shirt while another butts its head against Amir's leg. "I'll brush all of you!" Amir tells them, and I'm surprised to see how gentle his hands are.

"I'm exhausted!" London huffs loudly.

The girl with braids waves us over to a small area inside a low chain-link fence. There's a bench there, and a couple of trees. Plus one goat. "Why isn't he with his friends?" I ask as London and I sink down on the bench.

"He's recovering from an injury," the girl explains, patting the goat's head fondly.

I look closer. The goat is golden brown with black

patches on his back, and a torn left ear. I wince. "Poor baby! What happened?"

She grins. "Let's just say Marmalade loves to put his head in tight spots."

I grin back. "I'm Imaan," I say. "This is my friend London."

"Tamara," the girl replies. "I help my ma bring the animals here every week from our farm."

My eyes widen. I've never known anyone who lives on a farm. "What's it like?" I ask.

She shrugs. "Okay, I guess. There are lots of animals, and everyone in my family has chores. I have to wake up at five in the morning to help milk the cows before I can get ready for school. And there's no such thing as summer vacation. We're always working, twenty-four seven."

"Wow. That's dedication," London whispers. She's a big fan of hard work.

Me? Not so much. I'm suddenly thinking that helping Mama around the house isn't that big a deal. At least I can sleep late and take the summer off to laze around and have fun. "Sorry," I say to Tamara.

She gives me a grin. "It's a lot of fun too. You should come visit sometime. It's an amazing farm, we're very proud of it."

Just then, I hear a sneeze. My heart starts to thump in my chest like a drum. Was that Amir? Slowly, I turn to see him surrounded by goats, but he looks fine.

I'm distracted by Olivia walking up with the cat carrier and backpack. That's when I remember our actual job. Poor Bella, Missy, and Clyde must be seriously sick of being cooped up. Not to mention hungry and possibly poopy. "Can we let our kittens out here?" I ask Tamara. "We need to make sure they get playtime."

Tamara looks super curious, so of course London

pulls out a Must Love Pets flyer and talks up the business. Tamara seems really interested and asks lots of questions, like how long we've been pet sitting and how much we charge. Marmalade tries to eat a flyer, and there's a lot of tugging to get it out of his mouth.

"He thinks paper is fine cuisine," Tamara tells us apologetically.

"That's okay," I say. "We've got plenty of flyers."

Olivia and I carefully take the kittens out of the carrier, one by one, and put them on the ground. Soon, they're scampering around happily, pouncing on butterflies, eating blades of grass. They look so happy to be out. I want to stroke a finger down their heads, but I remember their biting and scratching from the day before. So I just lie back on the grass and let the sun warm my face.

It's so nice out here with my two favorite things: animals and friends.

Tamara's mom calls her from the main petting zoo enclosure. The crowd of kids wanting to pet animals is growing. Tamara looks at us and says, "I need to go help my ma. Can I trust you to take care of Marmalade?"

London looks at her sharply. But before London can say anything, Tamara adds, "I'll pay you for your services, of course."

And just like that, we have another pet-sitting client. Marmalade the Goat.

CHAPTER 12

Marmalade is a very strange goat. We spend only a few minutes pet sitting him before we figure out the two things he adores: paper and kittens.

"Stop, you . . . goat!" Olivia hisses for the twentieth time, as Marmalade pushes his face into her backpack and nibbles at the flyers inside.

"His name is Marmalade!" Amir screeches for the twentieth time. He's joined us on the grass now, his nose running and his hair all over his face like a hooligan.

Marmalade bleats, then lets himself be pushed away.

He's clever, though, because he's got a bunch of Must Love Pets flyers in his mouth.

"OMG, what's wrong with him?" I squeal. "Why does he want to eat those things?"

"Goats eat all kinds of weird stuff," Olivia says. "I read about it in one of my animal books."

Olivia knows a lot about animals. Some of her knowledge comes from books, but some is from real-life experience pet sitting her aunt's dog, Fifi.

I'm pretty sure she's got zero experience dealing with a goat, though.

We watch Marmalade chew through the flyers, leaving bits and pieces scattered about. London shoos him away and collects the paper carefully so the kittens don't eat it.

Uh-oh. Now Marmalade has discovered the kittens. He nudges Bella with his head, then Clyde. Missy runs under Marmalade's legs, and he turns to sniff at her.

Then he licks her right on the head.

Amir claps his hands in delight. "They're best friends!"

"It's love at first sight!" Olivia coos.

"Ew," I reply, but I'm smiling at this perfectly adorable picture.

Soon, Marmalade gets tired. He sits down on the ground, his head on his front legs, eyes closed. The kittens play around him, jumping on his back, clutching at his tail, rolling around in the grass right next to him. I can hear them purring happily.

Marmalade bleats a little bit, then goes quiet.

Maybe he's just enjoying the sun. And the friends.

All of a sudden I wish Baba were here. He'd totally be enjoying this scene. My smile dims a little, like it always does when I think of Baba and all the things he's missing.

All the things I'm missing because he's not here.

“Smile, Imaan!” Olivia calls out.

I look up. She’s taken out her camera and is clicking away. I smile at her. Then I smile at Amir, who’s sitting cross-legged on the grass, elbows on his knees. He’s watching the kittens run around like it’s better than his favorite cartoon. I think of what he said in the morning, about not remembering Baba anymore.

Click-click-click.

I shake my head firmly. No need to be sad when the day’s so wonderful.

Right?

Right.

At noon, London and I go back to the main market to check on Dada Jee. He’s still sitting on his folding chair, but he’s lost his grumpy face. The watermelon lady is sitting nearby, and she's laughing about something. On their other side is an older man selling apple pies, and he's also laughing.

Dada Jee isn't laughing, of course. I'm not sure he knows how to. But he's looking relaxed. And . . . happy?

I blink to make sure I'm seeing correctly.

Yup. Still relaxed and happy. It makes my heart grow big.

Even better, the lemons are half gone. There are still a lot on the table, but at least he sold some. Yay!

"Get some lunch, Imaan," Dada Jee says, giving me some cash. "For your friends too."

We wave as we walk away. Lunch sounds great right now.

That's when I see a big problem. It's really tough to choose what to eat when you're in a farmers' market. There are literally hundreds of choices. We finally choose fresh, puffy flatbread that looks like naan but topped with gooey cheese and olives.

We head back to the petting zoo loaded with food. Olivia and Amir literally clap when they see us. London finds hand sanitizer in her purse and passes it around, then we dig in like starving beasts. I can't even remember when I was ever this hungry before.

"Yum!" Amir mumbles. His mouth is so full, his cheeks are bulging.

"No veggies, see?" I tease.

"No veggies," he agrees.

I go back to stuffing myself. The flatbread is really delicious. I totally groan with happiness, just like Amir.

"I could use your granddad's lemonade right now," Olivia sighs when she's finished.

"I know!" I say. "I think he was scared to bring

any. Mama made such a big deal about him selling his lemons here."

London frowns. "Why? It's a good business decision."

"That's just it. Mama doesn't think he should start a business."

London frowns some more. "Why?" she asks again. I think she's shocked that someone wouldn't be okay with starting a business.

I lean my head against her shoulder for a second. "I . . . I'm not sure," I reply slowly. "I'm still trying to figure it out."

Olivia copies me, putting her head on London's other shoulder. "London can help," she says. "We all can."

I give them both grateful looks. "Thanks."

We get to our feet and start packing up. The kittens have been fed, and now they're playing all over Marmalade again. The goat bleats like he loves the attention.

Tamara comes back and pays us for the time we spent with her goat. "You three were excellent!" she exclaims. "Marmalade usually tries to escape at least twice, but he's been so happy with you all!"

I roll my eyes. "With the kittens, you mean."

She turns around and laughs. Missy has climbed all the way up Marmalade's back and is now standing on top of him like an explorer. "She's a climber," Tamara says admiringly.

I think of the curtains in my living room and nod.

"Why don't you kids go check out some of the carnival rides?" Tamara says. "The Tilt-A-Whirl is the best. You definitely need to try it."

"That's a great idea!" I reply. I'm expecting Amir to be excited, but he's quiet and his eyes are puffy. "Do you feel sleepy?" I ask him anxiously. He doesn't take a nap in the afternoon anymore, but sometimes I think he secretly wants to. "You can lie down on the grass here."

Amir rubs his eyes. "Don't want to."

"Carnival it is, then!" London says, clapping her hands.

We gather our things and put the kittens in the carrier. London leads the way with quick steps. Olivia takes pictures with her camera.

Tamara is right. The Tilt-A-Whirl is awesome! We take turns so that one of us girls is always with the kittens. By the time we're done, it's four o'clock and the market is officially closed. Dada Jee's waiting for us at his stall, a small grin on his face. We all stare at him. "What happened?" I ask breathlessly.

"I sold all my lemons!" he says, still grinning.

"OMG, that's awesome!" I cry, and hug him, not even caring that he may be embarrassed. He hugs me back. He looks so good now that the grumpy face is gone.

Then I realize why. He looks like Baba, only with more wrinkles and white hair. "I'm so proud of you, Dada Jee," I whisper.

"Me too, child," he replies.

CHAPTER 13

We end up walking home because Mr. Bajpai left in his van after lunch. It's a good thing Dada Jee sold all his lemons because carrying those heavy buckets home would have been torture.

Since they're empty now, I carry them stacked inside one another, dragging them behind me on the sidewalk. Lots of other people are carrying their empty carts and baskets the same way. I see the watermelon lady lugging a box behind her, and wave cheerfully.

"See you next week?" she asks.

I'm not sure, so I just shrug. It would definitely be nice to come to the market again. I can't wait to eat more deliciousness.

We're almost at the exit when Amir screeches to a halt. "We have to say good-bye to Marmalade!" he shouts.

"Who?" Dada Jee asks. "What?"

We turn in the opposite direction toward the petting zoo as Amir explains about Marmalade. "A goat, huh?" Dada Jee says. "We used to have goats on Bakra Eid every year when I was a child. I'd make friends with all of them and bring them treats to snack on."

London and Olivia want to know what Bakra Eid is. "*Bakra* is Urdu for 'goat,'" he tells us. "Eid-ul-Adha is a Muslim celebration in which we eat the goat meat, and share with our friends and neighbors. So sometimes it's known as Bakra Eid."

Amir laughs. "Goat Eid! That's funny!"

"Do you celebrate Eid here?" Olivia asks.

I nod. Eid is a very special time for Muslims. Mama and I always dress up in our fanciest shalwar kameez, and I put henna on my hands. "It's really fun," I reply. "No bakra, though."

"Too bad," London adds, laughing.

Tamara and her mom are packing up everything, and most of the goats are already in their transport trailer. Marmalade is standing to the side, nibbling at a pile of hay. When he sees us, he gives a very loud bleat and rambles up. "Hi, dude," Amir says, rubbing the goat's head. "I'm gonna miss you."

Marmalade bleats again. He nudges the cat carrier London's holding, like he knows his besties are in there. "Shh, they're sleeping, silly," London tells him, holding the carrier away from his face.

We pet him some more, then say good-bye to

Tamara. Olivia gives her some extra Must Love Pets flyers. Tamara gives us a brochure about her farm in case we want to visit. Her mom lets Amir brush Marmalade's coat one last time.

Finally, we go home. I say good-bye to London and Olivia on the street, then lug everything inside. Amir has to literally be pulled behind me because he's so tired. I know this because he keeps moaning, "Imaan, I'm tired. Help, Imaan!" like he's a zombie. He falls down on the carpet in the living room like he can't move another inch.

I hide my smile at his dramatics. Honestly, I just want to drop down beside him and snooze, but Responsible Imaan still has work to do. I put the lemon baskets in the garage and then try to convince Amir to get cleaned up. He needs to change out of those filthy clothes. I take a page out of Dada Jee's book and bribe him with chocolate chip cookies.

Amir runs upstairs ahead of me. Maybe our cookies are magical.

At least the kittens are still sleeping soundly, so that's one less thing to worry about. If I had to feed them or deal with their poop, I'd be one angry girl.

I'm eating dinner with my family when Mama notices Amir's puffy eyes. "What happened to you?" she demands. She's been quiet and broody ever since we got home.

Amir rubs his eyes as he eats chicken curry and basmati rice. "Nothing."

Mama turns to Dada Jee. "What happened? Why is his face like that?"

Dada Jee raises his bushy eyebrows. "Like what?"

I peer at Amir's face. It's not just the puffy eyes, I realize. His nose is red, like he's been rubbing it all day. And he keeps sniffing. "Amir, are you okay?" I ask.

He shrugs. "My eyes and nose itched all day."

I stare at him. I'm pretty sure my mouth is hanging open. "Why didn't you tell me?"

"I'm okay," he replies. "I'm not sneezing."

Mama makes a choking sound in her throat. "It could still be allergies. You don't have to be sneezing all the time."

"But there weren't any dogs around," I say, bewildered. When had Amir started looking so bad? Why hadn't I noticed?

A niggling feeling tells me why. I was too busy having fun at the farmers' market. Too busy spending time with my friends and a bunch of feisty animals to pay attention to my little brother.

Mama's looking at me closely, like she can tell what's running through my mind. "The doctor told us it could be anything. There's no way of knowing."

I hate not knowing, though. How will I ever

get my own dog if Amir keeps getting these stupid allergies and nobody can figure out what he's allergic to? I go back to my dinner, but while I chew, I'm also racking my brains, going over everything that happened today. The yummy pizzas, the kittens playing in the grass, the petting zoo . . .

"The goats!" I gasp. "Amir was brushing them when I heard a sneeze! It was you, wasn't it?"

"Their coat made my eyes itch," Amir informs us casually, like it's no big deal.

I try to think about this:

A. I'm relieved. At least it's not a dog allergy.

B. I'm sad. Poor Amir, miserable whenever he gets too close to animals.

"We'll do what London suggested," I finally say. "Make a report of every time you have a reaction. That way we can try to figure out what you're actually allergic to."

Amir brightens up. "Can I color the report?"

I give him a quick smile. He's such a silly goose. "Sure, why not?" I say. Mama is still looking freaked out, so I turn my smile on her and change the subject. "Did you know Dada Jee sold all his lemons? Isn't that wonderful?"

My plan backfires because Mama looks even madder. "Not really," she says. "These lemons are getting out of control. First it was the trees and the fertilizers. Then the harvest that went on and on. And now this selling business? It's no longer just a hobby!"

I want to tell her to chill out. All this anger isn't good for her, probably. But I think that may make her even angrier.

"So?" Dada Jee asks, standing up and leaning on his cane. His voice is loud, and the grin on his face from earlier in the day has disappeared totally. Like it wasn't even there. "Maybe I don't want a hobby anymore!"

Mama flings her napkin down on the table and makes another noise that sounds like *aaargh.*

I swallow. Mama and Dada Jee are always so polite to each other. So nice and friendly. Yeah, they're not really related, since Dada Jee was Baba's dad, not hers. But he is so important to our family. He's the one who takes care of us, cooks us delicious Pakistani dishes, spends time with us while Mama works.

He's the closest thing we have to Baba.

I hate them fighting. I'd do anything to make them stop.

But before I can say anything, Dada Jee shuffles out of the room with a grunt.

CHAPTER 14

"I don't get it," I say later that evening.

I'm kneeling in the middle of the living room floor, setting up a play area for Missy, Bella, and Clyde. It's an old playpen of Amir's from when he was a baby. I'd spied it in the garage when I put away Dada Jee's lemon buckets and dragged it out after dinner.

London and Olivia sit on either side of me, watching. "Get what?" Olivia asks.

I explain what happened at dinner between Mama and Dada Jee. "They've never fought before. They always say they're a team. Them versus us."

London shrugs. "Sometimes teams don't work well together."

She's right about that. Since Must Love Pets started, the three of us have often argued over how to do things. "But why?" I insist.

"Who knows?" London replies. "Adults are weird." She leans forward to examine the playpen. It's old and raggedy and so dirty. Ew. "That needs cleaning before we can put the kittens inside," she says.

I grab a pack of antibacterial wipes from the table nearby. "Already on it," I say.

The three of us take a wipe each and start cleaning. It's quiet for now. The kittens are eating their food inside the TV box Olivia brought from her house. I can hear them chomping and licking, which is totally funny. Amir's been dragged off for a bath by a frowning Mama, and Dada Jee's dozing in his armchair, a book on his lap. From the windows, I can see the sun dipping low in the horizon. It will be dark soon, but right now the sky is like a painting of pink and yellow.

"This is nice," I whisper.

"Why are you whispering?" Olivia asks, also whispering.

I giggle. "I don't know."

She giggles too. London rolls her eyes.

I'm just about to say something when I hear a loud rustling from outside, near our front door. Then there's a crash, as if something fell down hard.

Dada Jee snaps his eyes open and looks around. "What was that?"

London, Olivia, and I rush to the door. I peer through the side window and let out little scream. A big black eye with a rectangular pupil—*rectangular!*—is pressed up against the glass. I'm not sure what it is, or who it belongs to. My heart is jumping in my chest.

"What? What?" Olivia demands from behind me. Then she sees the big eye and squeals. "What *is* that?"

Before I can stop her, London throws open the door. "Oh, hello, Marmalade," she says.

I take deep gulping breaths to calm myself. "Marmalade?

"The bakra," Olivia says helpfully.

We all crowd outside on the front porch. The black eye definitely belongs to our friend from the farmers' market. Marmalade is butting his head into London's stomach, as if saying, *Hello to you too.* Or maybe he's saying, *I'm hungry, feed me.* I can't be sure. The big flowerpot that's always on the porch is now lying broken on the ground.

Dada Jee comes to the door, cane in hand. "Is this the goat from the market?" he demands, looking at us accusingly. "How did it get here?"

"How would we know?" I reply, offended. I look around like maybe Tamara will pop out from the bushes and yell, *Surprise!*

But there's no Tamara. "I guess he followed us home," Olivia finally says.

Is that even possible? How did we miss an animal trailing behind us as we walked home? And where has Marmalade been all this time? We got back at least three hours ago.

Dada Jee waves his cane around. "Well, we can't keep him, not with your mama already in a mood."

Right, Mama. I try not to think of what she'll say when she finds Marmalade here. And the broken flowerpot. "He's still a client, Dada Jee," I say. "We need to take care of him until we can figure out what to do."

London takes a deep breath. "Imaan's right. We'll figure it out."

Dada Jee crosses his arms across his chest. "Any ideas?"

"I'm thinking!" replies London.

Marmalade is now sniffing in the broken flowerpot, trying to eat Mama's roses. Yup, he's definitely hungry. I gently pull his collar and lead him to the patch of grass in the front yard. It's full of weeds, and I know goats love weeds. He bleats loudly as we go.

He also poops along the way. Ew. Ew. Ew.

"You better pick that up," Dada Jee remarks. "Before your mama . . ."

"I got it!" Olivia yells, already running back into the house to grab a plastic bag.

I don't wait for her. I watch as Marmalade chews on the weeds, my brain working overtime. Tamara and her mom must be so worried. Maybe they came back to the farmers' market to look for him. Maybe they called the police . . .

Wait, can you call the police for a missing goat?

"Tamara has our flyer. Maybe she'll call us," London says slowly.

Flyer? I turn toward her. Something about what she just said jogs my memory. "She gave me her info too, remember?"

London's eyes widen. "She did? When?"

I'm already running back inside. "Watch the goat, Dada Jee!" I yell.

I ignore his grumbling and rush into the living room. I stop short because Amir is sitting on the floor, the kittens all around him mewling and pawing like he's a giant playground for tiny baby animals. "Amir, why did you take them out of the box?" I almost shout. That's all we need right now, the kittens running around messing up the kitchen again.

Amir shakes his head. "I'm a perfect pet sitter," he

tells me proudly. "I brushed those goats all by myself today."

Mama pops her head out of the laundry room, a basket full of clothes under her arm. "And got allergies," she adds.

"Yes," Amir says, not even a little bit sorry.

Mama goes back into the laundry room, and I hear the washing machine start up. It's ancient, and very loud. *Rat-tat-tat.*

Not loud enough to drown out Marmalade's bleating, though. London points to the front door. "Hey, Amir, you'll never guess who's come visiting."

Amir leaps up and charges out at full speed. "Marmalade!" he screams at the top of his lungs. The kittens meow and follow him like loyal subjects.

I open my mouth to call him back, but London pulls my arm. "He'll be okay. Olivia and your granddad are outside." She gives me a look. "We're searching for something, remember?"

Oh, right. Tamara. "She gave me a brochure for her farm," I say. "I bet it has a phone number on it."

"Where is it?" London asks.

I look around wildly. I can't remember where I put it.

We search everywhere. The cat carrier. The backpack. Even the trash can. Just when I'm feeling the prick of tears behind my eyelids, London snaps her fingers. "Your jeans pocket. You're always putting things there and then forgetting all about them."

I sigh in relief that my best friend knows me so well. I start to smile. Then I see Mama from the corner of my eye, and I remember.

I threw my jeans in the laundry room before dinner.

The washing machine gives another loud rattle. *Too late. Too late.*

CHAPTER 15

Mama comes back out of the laundry room. She's on her phone now. "Yes, Mr. Greene, I think that's a great idea!"

She stops in front of the doorway to listen and nod. "Uh-huh. Yes, of course. If you hire me as your accountant, I'll be sure to help you with those issues."

"What's the deal with Mr. Greene?" London whispers to me.

I give her a wild look. Why are we talking about my neighbor right now? "Focus," I hiss as I brush past Mama and into the laundry room. Maybe my jeans aren't in the washing machine yet. Maybe Mama's washing bedsheets or something.

Nope. The laundry basket is empty. I take a quick peek in the machine and it looks full of Amir's and my clothes. Lots of denim. My heart sinks. "I think it's in there," I whisper to London.

London peers into the washing machine with me. "Water isn't good for paper, like, at all," she whispers back.

I don't even say *duh* like I normally would. Sometimes the obvious doesn't need to be said out loud.

"What are you girls looking for?" Mama sticks her head into the laundry room. Her phone is in her hand.

"Nothing," I reply in a low voice. That prick of tears is back behind my eyelids, and I don't turn around.

London does. "Imaan had a paper in her jeans

pocket," she explains. "Like a brochure, maybe. Did you see it?"

Mama sighs like she's not surprised. "On the shelf."

I look up at the shelf over the dryer so quickly my neck aches. Yes! There's a folded-up paper on it, just like the one Tamara handed to me. London grabs it before I can. "Thanks, Mrs. Bashir!"

I turn and hug her. "Thanks! You can't believe . . ."

Mama hugs me back, then puts up her hand. "No, please don't tell me. I've been trying to talk Mr. Greene into signing with me as a client. I'm really not in the mood to hear about your pet escapades right now."

Right. Maybe telling Mama about the goat eating weeds in our front yard isn't the best idea. I close my mouth and give her a tight-lipped smile. "Hope it works out with Mr. Greene."

"You and me both. His art business is getting

popular, and he can't handle the paperwork. He's almost decided to hire me, I can feel it."

"Good luck," London tells her.

"Thanks, dear." Mama smiles at us both and walks away, phone back at her ear.

I take the brochure from London and unfold it. It's glossy paper, full of pictures of a cute little farmhouse, a red barn, and animals in the grass. Chickens. Goats. Horses. There's even a picture of Tamara and her mom smiling as they work in the stables. The first panel says *Sweet Pea Farm*. I turn it over for contact information. Sure enough, there's an address and phone number at the back. "Bingo!"

I rush out to the hallway and pick up our landline.

"Imaan, we can't find Bella!" Amir rushes inside just as I've finished talking to Tamara on the phone.

I grit my teeth. Those wily kittens! I just want to sit down for five minutes. "What do you mean, you can't find Bella? Where is she? Why weren't you keeping an eye on her?"

He rushes back outside before I can ask more questions.

London and I look at each other in dread, then follow Amir outside. Dada Jee and Olivia are arguing in the front yard, pointing to something on the ground. "You haven't cleaned up properly," Dada Jee insists. "There's still some poop on the grass."

"That's just mud. I cleaned up really good already!"

I scan the yard quickly, trying not to freak out. It's no use. The animals are nowhere to be seen.

No Marmalade.

No Bella, Missy, or Clyde.

Nothing that resembles even one four-legged creature that's my responsibility to take care of. "What happened?" I say very loudly. "Where are the pets?"

Olivia looks up, startled. "They were just here, playing!"

I swallow. "They're not here, Olivia! You were supposed to be watching them!"

"No, I was supposed to be cleaning up since you never want to do it!"

"Me? How is this my fault? I wasn't even outside!" I'm yelling now, but I don't care. "I was calling Tamara to let her know her goat's here. You know, the one we're supposed to be taking care of? And then Carl messaged, asking if the kittens were okay, and I said yes, because how was I supposed to know they've totally disappeared?"

London puts a hand on my arm. "Calm down, Imaan. This isn't helping!"

I take a deep, trembling breath. Everyone is staring at me like I've totally lost my mind. Then

Mama comes running outside. "I heard shouting. What's going on?"

"The girls lost the animals," Dada Jee says.

"What?" I whirl to him. "You . . ."

He grunts, and I realize he's got a glint in his eye. "I'm teasing you, silly girl. It was my fault, I'm the adult here."

Olivia shakes her head. "They're too quick for us," she says. "Amir was playing with them, and I didn't think he needed supervision. They just . . . disappeared."

"Have you *met* my brother?" I ask. "He's, like, the kid who needs the most supervision on the planet."

Both Mama and Dada Jee grunt in agreement. Then Mama looks around. "Where *is* Amir?"

My heart sinks. Oh no. It's bad enough I lost my clients. If I lose my brother too, I will officially resign from Must Love Pets. Maybe even the Bashir family. I'm the worst pet sitter in the world.

And the worst big sister.

A small whimper escapes my lips. I clamp my jaw shut, but it's too late. London is glaring at me. She gives my arm another shake. "Stop feeling sorry for yourself," she says sternly. "They can't have gone far. Let's look."

"Good idea," Mama says. Then she ruffles my hair. "Don't worry, *jaan*."

I relax just a bit. If Mama's not freaking out, maybe it's okay. I look around, trying to think. There's movement behind a big tree in the corner of our yard. "There's Amir!"

We walk—run, really—to the tree. Amir is sitting on the ground, shoulders slumped, facing the fence between our yard and the neighbors'.

The fence with two pickets missing.

I stare at the gap. How had we never noticed

it before? It is the perfect size for kittens to pass through. Even a bigger animal—like a goat!—could squeeze through without much problem.

"They're gone," Amir tells us sadly. "They didn't want to play with me. They wanted to play in there."

I bend and peer through. I can't see much, but I can hear Marmalade bleating. And the kittens mewling. "They're definitely in there," I say in relief.

At least they're not lost, right?

Right.

Then I turn around and see Mama's horrified face. "That's Mr. Greene's house."

CHAPTER 16

Mama's starting to freak out, and it's a sight to see.

"I can't believe this!" she whisper-hisses, her face tight with anger. "Your kittens are in my potential client's yard. What are they doing there? How did they get out? And what's that sound?"

I gulp. "That's Marmalade."

"What?"

"Marmalade's a goat, Mama," Amir explains. "He's from the farmers' market."

"A . . . what? A goat?" Her whisper gets even lower, like she's a snake about to strike me dead.

"Are you serious, Imaan? We have three kittens and a goat invading our neighbor's yard? The same neighbor that I need to turn into a client so I can make a little more money? Is that what you're telling me right now?"

"Now, calm down . . ." Dada Jee begins.

Mama turns to him with narrowed eyes. "Don't tell me to calm down! This is your fault! You got so involved in selling your lemons, you forgot to take care of the kids. They've been running around wild with animals ever since summer break started!"

Dada Jee's eyebrows sink over his eyes. "My fault?"

"Yes! I told you not to start selling lemons. I told you not to turn this hobby into something else . . ."

And just like that, Mama's anger at me has turned to Dada Jee. She's standing with her legs apart and her hands on her hips. Classic fight mode. I need to shut it down fast, before things get worse.

Only I'm not sure how to do that. This has literally never happened before. The united front these two always have is crumbling like tissue paper before my eyes. It's . . . scary. Ugh, I wish Baba was here. He'd know what to do. He's the link that keeps Mama and Dada Jee together.

"Now look here, Amna . . ." Dada Jee begins, his voice rumbling in his chest.

I look at London and Olivia pleadingly. Surely, they have some ideas. Olivia shrugs helplessly. London rolls her eyes.

"Uh, Mrs. Bashir?" London interrupts very bravely.

"What?" Mama snaps, but her tone is less angry now. She takes a breath. "Sorry, London, dear. What do you need?"

London waves to the hole in the fence. "We need to go get the animals."

Mama closes her eyes, then opens them again and deeply exhales. "Yes, of course. You're absolutely right."

I breathe a sigh of relief. Okay. Mama's coming back to her senses. Things will get back to normal now. Right?

Wrong.

Mama calmly leans forward until she's really close to the fence. Then she grips the picket next to the missing ones. I open my mouth to ask what she's doing when there's a ripping sound, and she's pulled the picket right off the fence.

"Mama!" I gasp.

Mama doesn't respond. She repeats the action with the next picket, and then the one after that. Soon, there's a big gap in the fence.

We all stare at the fence, horrified and silent. "Go on," Mama says, pushing me forward. "Go get those animals before Mr. Greene finds out."

"Why couldn't we have gone to his front door?" Dada Jee demands, frowning. "What sort of example are you setting here?"

Mama shakes her head. "If I knock on his door, he'll know what's going on. Then he'll think I'm unprofessional and never become my client."

"Still . . ."

"This is our fence too," Mama says. "Do you have a better idea?"

Dada Jee's frown gets darker. "Yes! Go ring the doorbell and tell him what's happening. He's fought in a war. He's not going to be scared of tiny kittens and a paper-eating goat."

Mama and Dada Jee glare at each other like they're the worst enemies. My heart is shriveling up inside.

What happened to teammates? What happened to us versus them?

"I agree," Olivia says in a low voice. "We should just ring his doorbell."

Mama says, "*Aargh*" and stalks away to the neighbor's front door. The lights go on, and we can hear her explaining something. Then we hear a grumpy voice. Mr. Greene.

"He sounds angry," Olivia says nervously.

"Nonsense," Dada Jee replies. "Let me talk to him. Veteran to veteran."

The three of us follow Dada Jee. At the last minute, I haul Amir up and bring him with us. Who knows what he'll get up to if he's alone?

"Hey!" he protests, all innocent.

"Hush!" We power walk to Mr. Greene's house. The poor man can't understand what's going on. He's sputtering and waving his hands around as

Dada Jee and Mama try to talk to him. It's not going well. The frowns are getting bigger, and the voices are getting louder.

"Your kittens are in my backyard?" Mr. Greene asks for the third time.

"And a goat," Mama says, looking like she's about to die of embarrassment.

"A goat?" he repeats slowly. "I thought you were an accountant, but apparently you're running a farm."

Mama looks miserable.

"Sheesh," I say, looking at the sky. The sun is setting now, and before we know it the light will fade. That will make it a hundred times harder to find those slippery animals. "Can we just go get the animals before they disappear again?"

Everyone looks at me in alarm. "Good idea," Mr. Greene says, and opens his front door wide enough for all of us to troop in. "But don't touch anything!"

Mama nods and snatches Amir's hand in hers so that he doesn't accidentally bump into anything. Like silent soldiers, we pass the living room and kitchen. Everything is neat and tidy, with none of the personal things I'm used to, like pillows or flower vases. I have more questions about Mr. Greene now. Does he live alone? Where is his family? Does he miss them?

Mr. Greene leads us through the kitchen door into the backyard. It's almost as big as ours, the only difference being a big white shed in the corner. In the low light, I can make out a hand-painted sign on the shed wall: GREENE'S PHOTOS.

This must be where he runs his business. His storage for the Etsy store. His workshop. His office.

I get a shiver down my back as I look around. The backyard is empty. No goat. No kittens. But the door to the shed is wide open.

Should it be open?

The biggest lesson I've learned from Must Love Pets: Never, *ever* leave a door open if there are animals around.

Actually, this also goes for young pesky siblings like Amir the Curious, but that's a different story.

Mr. Greene apparently knows about this lesson too. He heads to the shed with a grim look on his face. "I was working here when you rang the bell," he tells Mama. "I didn't lock up."

"You should always lock up," Mama says faintly. "You never know who'll sneak inside and mess things up." She's staring at the open door like she doesn't want to know what's inside. Or if anything is messed up.

Neither do I.

I have a very bad feeling that everything we're looking for will be inside that little shed.

And it will be a disaster.

CHAPTER 17

Mr. Greene strides into the shed. Mama and Dada Jee follow close behind. All us kids crowd around, craning our necks to see inside.

Honestly, I'm scared to see. But I figure it's my job, since I'm the person who thought Must Love Pets was a good idea. And because I'm in customer service. According to *Shark Tank*, that's very important when things are going badly. London would be proud of me for remembering that.

I'm scared to look, but I peek into the shed with the others and glance anyway.

It is definitely a disaster.

On the ground in the middle of the shed lies a pile of broken frames. Marmalade is chewing on paper sticking out from the frames. He doesn't even care that he could get hurt from the broken glass.

Mr. Greene makes a growl in his throat, like he's an injured tiger. "Shoo!"

Marmalade totally ignores him. He's in paper heaven, his jaw chewing, his eyes half closed.

"Oh my," Mama whispers. "What . . . how?"

I look away from the mess on the floor, trying to locate the kittens. The shed walls are covered in shelves full of black-and-white pictures of nature. Forests. Lakes. Deserts. There's even a meadow full of wildflowers. I know they're probably amazing, but this is not the time to admire them.

Olivia points to the wall in front of us. Missy, Bella, and Clyde are walking about on the top shelf, ears perked, tails straight up in the air. Clyde swipes a paw at a picture of a tree, and it teeters at the edge of the shelf. My heart is in my throat as I watch.

"The kittens are throwing things down." Olivia states the obvious.

Mr. Greene makes another noise. This time he sounds scared. "My pictures," he groans. "They'll all be destroyed."

Something in his face pushes me into action. "No, they won't!" I say. I squeeze under Dada Jee's arm and step inside the shed. "We'll take care of this."

London follows me, then Olivia. They grab Marmalade by the collar and begin to pull him gently away from the mess on the floor. He bleats in protest. "Come on, your owner will be here soon," London tells him firmly.

I scan the shed. There's a stepladder in the corner near the window. Perfect! I'm a pro at climbing ladders and saving kittens by now! I grab the ladder and bring it over to where the kittens are. Quickly, I climb up. If I stretch my arm all the way, I can reach the top shelf. The ladder wobbles a little bit, and I clutch a shelf.

"Careful," Dada Jee warns. Mama's just watching, with a half-panicked, half-proud look on her face. I give her a little smile to tell her it's okay, then turn back to the shelf.

I click my tongue. "Here, kitties!"

The kittens stare at me like I'm being very rude.

I click my tongue again, and finally Missy comes over to investigate. "Come here, you silly girl!" I pluck her from the shelf and hand her down to Olivia.

She mews loudly like I betrayed her or something.

Clyde and Bella are too far. I wave my hand toward them a few times, but they know what I'm doing. They slink even closer to the pictures. Drat. I'll have to think of something else.

I rack my brains. Then I remember how I got Missy down from our living room curtain. "Go get a toy from our house, Amir!" I shout.

"On it!" he shouts back. "I'll go through the fence like a superhero!"

"Through the fence?" Mr. Greene repeats.

I'd forgotten about the hole Mama made in the in-between fence. "We'll talk about it later," Mama promises.

Amir is back in a minute, holding a bunch of cat toys in his arms. He hands me the pink mouse, and I dangle it in front of Clyde and Bella. They act like I'm not even there. "Give me something else," I say.

Amir hands me a yellow bird with bright purple feathers. "Try this."

Perfect! Cats love chasing birds, don't they?

Hopefully they're too young to realize that no actual bird here has bright purple feathers.

I hold the toy out and move it around fast. *Swish-swish.* Clyde swipes a paw at it, then moves toward me just a little. "Come on," I whisper, swishing again. "You know you want this!"

It works. Clyde and Bella both lunge forward to get the bird. I'm smarter and faster, though. I drop the bird and grab one kitten in each hand.

They yowl and twist.

I yowl too because at least one of them claws me pretty bad. "Naughty kittens!" I gasp. But I don't let go. Olivia's already holding Missy, so I look around for another person. "Here, Dada Jee."

Dada Jee looks startled. "Me?"

I push Bella toward him, and he takes her. Gently.

Mama holds out her arms. "Give me the other one,"

she says. I hand over Clyde, and she picks him up by supporting his back legs just like you're supposed to.

Mr. Greene looks at us like he can't understand what's going on. "Are there any more of these evil creatures?" he asks.

I grin at him and climb down from the stepladder. "Nope, we got all of them!"

He opens his mouth to say something else, but there's a movement at the doorway. It's London, holding the cat carrier. "Good job, team!" she says, also grinning.

We place the kittens in the carrier. They're tired after all the excitement and lie down immediately. "Don't open the door, mister!" I tell Amir.

He nods and sniffs. I think his eyes are itching again.

Dada Jee takes him by the hand. "Let's get home, shall we?" he says. "You should have been in bed by now."

"Can I have a cookie?" Amir asks as they walk away.

"Only if you change into your pajamas in less than five minutes," Dada Jee replies. "No funny business."

Amir perks up. "Get out your stopwatch!"

When they're gone, I turn to London again. "Where's Marmalade?"

"Tamara's dad came to get him," she replies.

I sigh gratefully. We all stand there for a minute, taking deep breaths. I'm happy that all Must Love Pets' clients are finally safe and accounted for.

But this problem is bigger than our clients. There's the mess in Mr. Greene's shed. There's Mama looking upset and worried.

I'm not sure what to do.

I think of Baba, like I always do when I need some life advice. *Just get things done*, he'd always say. *Don't think too much about it*, jaan.

I can do that.

I kneel near the broken frames and the half-eaten pictures on the floor. "Let's clean up, Must Love Pets team!"

London and Olivia crouch next to me. We carefully put the broken glass in a pile. Mama finds a trash can in the back of the shed and fills it with the glass.

I pick up a picture, which is tattered by goat teeth. It looks like a sunset on the ocean. "This is so beautiful," I whisper.

Mr. Greene shakes his head angrily. "These pictures were going on my Etsy store tomorrow morning," he says, his voice hard.

My heart starts to thump, and I look at Mama nervously. This is it. He's going to yell at us and say he never wants to work with Mama now. I wouldn't blame him. If my neighbors had animals invading my property and destroying my work, I'd be pretty mad too.

"I'm so sorry," Mama says in a low voice. "I don't know what to say."

"Hmmph!"

"Don't say anything," Olivia interrupts excitedly. She's staring at another chewed-up picture in her hand. "Maybe I can help."

CHAPTER 18

I'm dying to know what Olivia's brilliant plan is, but she's disappeared.

She told us to wait and that she'd be right back.

So, we wait.

It's awkward just standing around, so London and I continue the cleanup. Mama taps her foot on the ground and checks her watch again and again. Mr. Greene just looks grumpy and sad, all mixed up together.

We've cleared up all the broken glass and wrapped up all the pictures before Olivia comes back. She's holding her camera aloft like it's a trophy. "Here!" she says, grinning. "This is the solution."

I frown a little because I have no idea why she's brought her camera out. Does she think Mr. Greene wants his picture taken right now?

Mr. Greene is obviously puzzled too. "Nice camera," he says slowly. "But I don't really need it. I have three of my own."

Three? Wow. Who needs that many cameras?

Olivia nods like it's perfectly normal for one person to have so many fancy cameras. "I know," she replies. "But this is the camera that will help you today."

Mr. Greene's eyebrows meet on his forehead. "What do you mean?" he growls. "Nobody can fix this mess. I'll just lose business and won't be able to afford an accountant." He says this last part with a scowl at Mama, like everything is her fault.

I don't like that because Mama is completely

blameless in this disaster. The only culprits are the cutie pies named Bella, Missy, Clyde, and Marmalade.

Well, maybe also Amir for letting the kittens get loose. Again.

Oh, and the three of us for not being more responsible.

Ugh. This is brutal. Maybe Must Love Pets was a bad idea. My bad idea. If anyone's to blame, it's me, Imaan Bashir.

I feel miserable, but I look at Mama, and she looks way worse. Tired and irritated and miserable.

"What's your solution?" she prompts quietly, like she's just humoring Olivia. Or maybe trying to distract Mr. Greene and calm him down.

Only that's not gonna work. Mr. Greene's scowl is downright scary.

Olivia is fearless, though. "Mr. Greene, you take photographs of nature, right?" she continues.

Mr. Greene grunts. I guess that's a yes.

"This camera contains photographs of nature too," she says, waving the camera around again. "Animals, to be precise."

"Animals?" I ask, remembering the photos she showed us the other night. "You mean the kittens? And Marmalade?"

Now Mama looks less tired and more annoyed. "We don't want to hear any more about those four clients of yours!"

"Just look at them, please," Olivia says. "I take good pictures, I promise."

She holds out the camera so that the LCD screen faces Mama and Mr. Greene. I don't need to look because I've already seen the fantastic pictures Olivia takes.

"Oh my," Mama murmurs. "This looks like a tiger. That's one of your kittens?"

"It's Clyde," she says proudly.

Mr. Greene leans closer to the LCD. "This is really good quality," he says quietly. He's totally lost the scowl. "You know a lot about light and shadow."

Olivia blushes. I know she's happy about the praise, since Mr. Greene is an actual professional. "Thanks," she replies shyly.

She clicks through the pictures she's taken. There are lots from the farmers' market. Marmalade, but also the other goats at the petting zoo. A donkey eating a mouthful of grass. A group of cows with a sign behind them that says MILK. I'm totally shocked because I didn't even know she was taking all these pictures today.

"These are really good, Olivia," London whispers.

Everyone agrees with *hmmms* and *aaahs*.

Finally, Olivia puts away her camera. "So, what

do you think, Mr. Greene?" she asks. "Can you use any of these for your Etsy store? It would be our way of making up for all this destruction."

Mr. Greene rubs a hand over his mustache. "Well, if I blow up a few of these pictures, maybe in black and white, then frame them . . ."

"What do you think?" Mama asks.

"Well," he replies. "I'll have to see the enlarged photos when they're printed out."

"And you know how to do that?"

Mr. Greene looks at her like it's a trick question. "Of course. I do that every day." He turns to Olivia. "Can I keep your storage drive for the night? I'll transfer the pictures I'm interested in to my computer, and then print them out."

Olivia quickly takes her SD card out and hands it to him. "Can I see them when they get printed?"

He almost smiles. Almost. "Yes. And I'll also

add your name to the description on the website, so everyone knows who took these pictures."

Olivia squeals with delight. "OMG! That will be awesome!"

London and I squeal too.

Mr. Greene's mustache stretches. Wow, I think that is a genuine smile! I didn't know he had it in him. "No promises," he reminds us, but I don't think Olivia is really listening.

The three of us meet in a group hug, Olivia's camera between us like a precious football. "Good job, bestie!" I whisper in her ear.

Olivia beams.

Mama grips my elbow. "Let's leave Mr. Greene in peace now, kids." She starts to walk out, pulling me gently with her. London and Olivia follow arm in arm.

Mr. Greene clears his throat. "I'll call you tomorrow, Mrs. Bashir."

Mama and I look at each other. We have no idea what that means. Will he hire her? Or will he think she's not capable of doing a good job because some kids' animals got loose in his shed?

I want to give him a lecture, but Mama grips my elbow harder and practically drags me away.

"Sure, take your time," she replies, and we leave as fast as we can.

CHAPTER 19

That night, I sit at the kitchen table and eat strawberry ice cream. I feel like it's the best thing to do after all the drama today. Dada Jee is in his armchair, watching an Urdu comedy show on television. He shakes his head at the jokes, and waves his cane at the screen whenever something silly happens. "Who wrote this rubbish?" he asks me more than once.

I just shrug and eat my ice cream. I know he's having fun even though he's complaining.

Mama comes down the stairs and sinks down on

the couch in the living room. "That playpen looks great," she tells me. I'd finished cleaning it up after London and Olivia went home. Bella, Missy, and Clyde now sleep inside, curled up together on one of Amir's old blankets. I even cleaned up their litter box without too much gagging.

I deserve a prize for that alone.

I get Mama a bowl of ice cream and sit down next to her. She looks tired.

"Do you think Mr. Greene is still mad at us?" I ask.

She eats a spoonful of ice cream and sighs. "I hope not. It was just a few pictures. Not the end of the world."

Dada Jee switches off the TV and turns to us. "Just a few pictures?" he demands. "It's the guy's business. It means a lot to him."

Mama frowns. "You think you know everything

about running a business just because you've sold a few buckets of lemons?"

She says it very quietly, but I hear it. "Mama!" I whisper, shocked. That is *so* not how one talks to elders in our house.

Dada Jee frowns too. "What did she say about my lemons?"

Great. They're fighting again. This is definitely not what I want to hear after all that's happened today. Why can't they be nice to each other? What is happening?

Mama opens her mouth to reply. I stand up quickly and hold up a hand. "Stop!"

They both look at me, startled. I'm breathing heavily, and my hands are clenched at my sides. "Stop!" I repeat, louder this time. "You two need to stop fighting. I . . . I don't like it!"

Mama and Dada Jee are staring at me like they've

never seen me before. I guess it's because I've never stood up and shouted at them before. "You two have always been a team," I whisper. "You can't fight like this all the time."

"We're not fighting, exactly," Mama says. "I just disagree with your grandfather's plans for starting a lemon business. Or whatever he wants to call it."

"But . . . but why?" Dada Jee growls. "How is it hurting you, Amna, if I sell a few lemons at the farmers' market?"

I wait for her answer. It's something I want to know too. Why is Mama so against it?

She sits back and closes her eyes. "I called you to America to help me with the kids," she says softly. "After Zahid died, I was alone. I needed you."

This guts me. My anger flies away and I sink down beside her. She looks so young and sad. She never talks about Baba, and it's easy to forget that she must miss him even more than I do.

Dada Jee must be thinking the same thing. He lets out a big sigh and says, "I'm always here for you, my dear daughter. My first priority is always going to be the kids. Have I been doing a bad job with them?"

Mama shakes her head. "No. You're great with them. We're so lucky to have you."

I nod because this is 100 percent true. London's grandparents live in Connecticut, and she's always saying she wishes they were closer. I'm so glad Dada Jee lives with us. I'm so glad he left his home in Pakistan and moved to California for us. He's the missing link between us and Baba.

Mama sighs and leans her head against the back of the couch. "I guess, maybe, somehow . . . I feel jealous of your lemons."

There's a weird silence as we all digest this. I'm

not sure Mama meant to say that out loud. "Jealous?" I squeak. "Of lemons?"

Mama sighs again. "Of the time they take. All the care that goes into growing them. The harvesting. The selling."

I stare at her. I suddenly know what she means. What if the lemons become more important than us?

Dada Jee is thinking hard too. I can tell from the way his eyebrows are bunched up on his forehead. "The lemons are a connection to my homeland," he says. "They're a reminder of my family orchards in Pakistan. They're not just a hobby. They're a part of me."

Mama opens her eyes and straightens up. "Wait, I never realized you're lonely here."

Dada Jee shakes his head. "Not lonely. Just homesick sometimes. It's so different from what I grew up with."

I reach over and hug him because now he's looking sad too.

He hugs me back tightly, and presses a kiss on the top of my head. "I love Imaan and Amir," he continues after he lets me go, "but I want to have more in my life. Maybe a lemon business. Maybe something else. I don't know. But I do want to try."

I understand perfectly. My friends and I started Must Love Pets for a different reason, but the result is the same: taking a risk at something new. It's fun and exciting, even if you're not sure you're going to succeed.

"You should go ahead and try, Dada Jee," I tell him. "Right, Mama?"

Mama thinks for a second, then nods. "Yes, you should. It's your decision. I won't say anything to stop you anymore."

Dada Jee frowns some more. "Are you sure? No more shouting about my lemons?"

"No."

"And no more grumbling when there are buckets lying around?"

"Well, if you leave them lying around like you always do . . ."

I roll my eyes. "He can be more careful. Right, Dada Jee?"

He pretends to think about it. "Okay, sure. I'll keep them in the garage at all times."

"Perfect!" Mama and I say together. Then we burst out laughing.

Dada Jee grunts. "Good, because I sold a lot of lemons today at the farmers' market. Seems like my business is off to a great start!"

"Ooh, maybe you can sell lemonade next week," I say. "People always love that."

Dada Jee picks up the remote and switches the TV back on. "I'm glad you think so. You and your giggly friends will be helping me make gallons of lemonade next week."

I groan. "Seriously? What if we have more pet-sitting clients?"

He shrugs. "So what? You three are professionals, right?"

Mama snorts a little. I give her an offended look. "Right," I say firmly. Because I really think we are.

CHAPTER 20

London and Olivia arrive the next morning for a last play session with the kittens. Now that we have a playpen, the kittens don't seem like dangerous criminals on the loose, trying to destroy everything in their path.

"They're adorable." Olivia sighs, peering over the edge of the playpen. "Like soft little fluff balls."

"Fluff balls with claws and teeth," London replies. "But yeah, adorable."

I smile. Missy and Clyde are rolling around

together and pawing each other. Bella is crouched low next to them, trying to pounce on their tails.

Amir comes and stands with us. "Why are they fighting?" he wails. "They're supposed to be best friends."

Olivia ruffles his hair. "That's play-fighting," she tells him. "It's their way of learning."

"Learning what?"

"Well, they're animals, right? They need to learn how to catch their prey, and how to take care of themselves in the wild."

"The wilds of Amir's baby pen!" I say dramatically. "The most dangerous of environments!"

"Hey!" Amir protests, even though he has no idea what I just said.

"Hey yourself, silly goose!" I say. "Now tell me, which one's your favorite?"

He watches the kittens for a minute, his forehead

scrunched up in a very cute way. I'm glad he's not rubbing his eyes anymore. I'd made notes on his allergic reaction yesterday in a special file labeled AMIR'S ALLERGIES. So far we have dogs and goats on the list. I try not to think about what else will be added in the future.

"I can't decide," Amir finally admits. "I love all of them."

"Me too," I tell him, giving him a hug.

London leans over to rub a finger over one soft kitty head. A loud purring sound fills the air, and it makes me smile. "I'm really missing Marmalade right now," London says.

"Maybe we can go to the farmers' market again with Dada Jee next week," I say. "Tamara said we should stop by."

"That would be perfection," Olivia adds.

"Perfection," I repeat.

Soon, the kittens stop play-fighting and start to explore the playpen. "I think they're getting bored," London remarks.

"We can't have that!" I pick Missy up and turn to Amir. "Wanna play?"

Amir cheers and settles down on the carpet with Missy in his lap. I give him a few toys to keep her occupied.

"Me too!" Olivia says. She picks up Clyde in one hand and Bella in the other. She and London sit down next to Amir, making a circle with their bodies. The kittens play on their laps and on the floor in the middle. There's lots of mewling and sniffing from the animals, and lots of laughter from the humans.

I watch them happily. At one point, Amir looks up at me and smiles the biggest smile. My heart melts a little. There's a pressure in my chest, like I'm proud or something. *I did this,* I think. I got the idea of a pet-sitting business and brought joy to my friends and family. It doesn't matter if the animals only stay with us for a few days. And it definitely doesn't matter if things go horribly wrong—like a dog going missing or a goat eating a neighbor's property—because we eventually get them right. Plus, we always have so much fun doing it.

"All's well that ends well," comes a gruff voice from my side. It's Dada Jee, leaning on his cane. "That's from Shakespeare," he adds.

I roll my eyes at him. "You want to play with them?"

He gives a mock shiver. "No, thank you. The army vet is coming over for lemonade."

My eyes widen. "Mr. Greene's coming over?" I squeak. "Are you friends with him now?"

"Friends?" Dada Jee seems to be thinking about this. "Maybe."

Olivia looks up at us. “Maybe he has an update about my pictures,” she says quietly. “I hope he doesn’t hate them.”

I remember how impressed Mr. Greene had looked last night when Olivia showed him her camera. “Not a chance,” I say cheerfully.

Mr. Greene knocks on the back door after lunch. “The fence has a hole in it,” he says as a greeting.

Mama’s washing dishes at the sink. She turns quickly and wipes her hands on a dish towel. “Yes, I’ve called someone to fix it later today,” she says.

Dada Jee waves him to the kitchen table. “Come sit, have some lemonade.”

“Don’t mind if I do.”

We try not to stare as the two men sit side by side. Their feet are stretched out, and they’re drinking lemonade as they talk about the war. Mr. Greene looks relaxed. Not at all like a man whose precious art has been destroyed by a paper-obsessed goat and three naughty kittens. Maybe Shakespeare's right. All *is* well now that things are back to normal.

When he's finished with his drink, Mr. Greene turns to Olivia and hands her a big yellow envelope. "Your pictures."

Olivia's hands shake as she opens the envelope. In it are three big black-and-white photos. Two are of the kittens in various poses. One is of the group of cows from the farmers' market. "I still need to frame them," Mr. Greene says gruffly. "But I think they'll fit very nicely in my Everyday Nature collection."

Olivia doesn't say anything. She seems to be frozen, with her eyes stuck on the photos she's holding in her hands.

I give her a one-sided hug. London does the same from the other side. "You're so talented, Olivia," I tell her, grinning.

"Uh-huh," she stutters. I think she's in shock.

Mr. Greene takes the pictures back from her gently. "I need to get your parents' agreement that I can use your work," he says. "And I'll pay you a portion . . ."

"No!" Olivia finally finds her voice. "I don't want any payment for these. It's a gift from Must Love Pets because your work was ruined by our clients."

London and I nod. I realize we didn't actually apologize on behalf of Marmalade and the kittens last night. "We're sorry for everything," I tell him. "We'll take better care of our clients from now on."

Mama smiles at me, and mouths, *Proud of you!*

I smile back. That pressure in my chest is even bigger now. It makes me warm and happy.

Mr. Greene turns to Mama. She ducks her head, like she knows what's coming next. I think she's already decided he's not going to hire her. But Mr. Greene just says, "I'm looking forward to working with you," like it's no big deal.

Proud of you! I mouth back at her.

Mama's shoulders loosen, and she nods gratefully. Our grumpy neighbor sure likes making people speechless.

I flash him a smile. "Wanna say good-bye to our kittens, Mr. Greene? Their owner will be here soon."

Now he's the one who's speechless. "Um . . . well . . ."

I bite my lip. The idea of this big tattooed guy playing with cute little fluff balls is really hilarious. Dada Jee slaps Mr. Greene on the shoulder to get him moving. "Let's go!"

We're almost to the living room when the doorbell rings. It's Carl, looking exhausted but happy. "How did it go?" he asks.

London pulls him inside. "Have some lemonade while we tell you all about it," she says.

I follow them, but the phone rings. The Must Love Pets line. I wait until everyone's walked away, then pick up and say with my nicest voice, "Thank you for calling. How can we help your pet today?"

MUST LOVE PETS

Turn the page for a special sneak peek of *Bunny Bonanza*!

CHAPTER 1

"Strawberry and kiwi shouldn't go together, but they totally do," I declare.

I'm slouched in a shiny red seat at my favorite café, Tasty, with my favorite people, my besties, London and Olivia. In my hand is the best smoothie known to mankind: strawberry kiwi. At Tasty, they're served in tall glasses with thick paper straws.

Very fancy, right?

It's not just the smoothies, though. Everything about this café is dreamy and pastel-colored, like you've stepped through a magical portal or something. I could stay here forever.

"I prefer Berry Berry Wild," London says, wrinkling her nose. She's not a big fan of kiwi.

Olivia slurps noisily through her straw. "I think I agree."

I pretend to glare at her. "Traitor!"

Olivia sticks her smoothie-coated tongue out at me.

"Ew, gross!" I cry. "Amir's rubbing off on you!" Amir is my six-year-old brother and the king of grossness. Olivia adores him, which I kinda get because he's super adorable when he wants to be.

Still, eating with his mouth wide open is a signature Amir move. Disgusting.

My disgust makes Olivia even bolder. She leans closer and crosses her eyes. "What's gross about me, huh, Imaan? Huh?"

"You're weird," I tell her, trying not to laugh. She knows I don't really mean it, even though we haven't known each other very long. She and her family moved into the neighborhood just a few weeks ago. Now we're not only best friends, but also business partners in a pet-sitting company called Must Love Pets.

Olivia may be awesome, but she's also weird. A good kind of weird.

She sits back, arms across her chest. "Weird because I like berries?"

"Berries are the strangest!" I insist. "Like blueberries, so tart they shouldn't even be a fruit! And raspberries have those tiny hairs on them. What's up with that?"

Olivia's eyes widen. "Kiwi literally have hairy skin!"

I shrug and sip some more smoothie. "But they're delicious."

London throws a wrapper at me. She hates it when people argue in front of her. "Stop, you children!"

Olivia and I grin at each other. "Sorry, Mom!" I say. Unlike Olivia, I've known London forever. Since we were babies, to be exact. I don't even remember our first meeting. We were probably in diapers.

Ew, why did I just think of that? I hate anything poop-related, which isn't ideal for someone taking care of animals.

Olivia is slurping her smoothie almost like a challenge. I turn to her and whisper, "You know I'm right. Strawberry kiwi would win all the awards!"

"Oh yeah?"

"Yeah!"

We stare at each other, fighting our grins. Then we both pick up our glasses and clink them together like we're fancy ladies. "Cheers!" she says.

"Go for the berries—see if I care!" I reply.

"You two should have a competition," London muses. "Take a survey and see how many people like each smoothie. It's called market research."

I put my fist next to my ear, pretending to be on the phone. "Hey, London, *Shark Tank* called. They said they already have enough actual sharks, thank you very much!"

London glares at me. She's a huge *Shark Tank* fan and probably the only person who watches the show with pen and notepad in hand. Olivia and I dissolve into giggles at London's fierce expression.

"I could be a shark one day," London mutters.

I stop laughing and give her a sideways hug. "Definitely," I assure her. If anyone can grow up to be an amazing entrepreneur one day, it's London. She knows so much about business, it's unreal. Plus, she wears smart suit jackets with the sleeves rolled up like a boss lady.

We start talking about the latest *Shark Tank* episode. We watched it together at London's house two days ago. It was a lot of fun, even though I only understood about 60 percent. London translated the rest of the 40 percent in easy fifth-grade language.

Olivia finishes her smoothie and starts taking pictures of Tasty on her fancy camera. The red booths. The wood tables. The plate of cookies we're sharing. *Click-click-click.*

"Show me," I say, leaning over her shoulder to look at the LCD display. Olivia is really shy about her photography, but I want her to be proud of it. Her pictures saved us from a total disaster when some naughty kittens we were pet-sitting destroyed our neighbor Mr. Greene's art. Olivia offered to give him a few of her pictures to sell in his Etsy store in exchange for the ones he lost.

Taking care of animals is no joke. Sometimes it

gets downright stressful being co-owners of Must Love Pets. Our goal was to convince Mama that I'm responsible enough for a dog, but somehow every new client is Trouble with a capital T.

Olivia scrolls through the pictures. "Live action shots are the best."

"Like the kittens," I say, still thinking of the mischievous trio. Their names were Missy, Clyde, and Bella, and they were hilarious.

Olivia finds a picture of Amir sitting on the floor. The kittens are all over him like he's a jungle gym. "Amir is just as adorable as the kittens." Olivia giggles.

"Not really," I say, rolling my eyes. Amir is a pain in the behind. But I admit that the picture is cute.

"You should frame this one," London says.

Olivia shrugs. "Maybe."

I already know she's never going to do it. London and I exchange looks. I wag my eyebrows. It's my mission to make Olivia proud and excited about her pictures. I just have to think of the perfect way to do it so she doesn't get embarrassed or mad.

Piece of cake.

"Hello," comes a familiar voice behind us. We turn around, already smiling.

It's Angie, the tall, brown-haired owner of Tasty. She's wearing a pink-and-white-striped apron with the words QUEEN OF THE KITCHEN on it. "What a lovely camera, new girl," she continues.

New girl—ahem, Olivia—smiles shyly. "Thanks. It was a gift from my dad."

"Do you take good pictures?" Angie asks.

Olivia's shrugs. "They're okay."

"They're incredible!" I jump in. "She's a great photographer. Some of her pictures are selling on Etsy."

"Really?" Angie looks very impressed. "Well, all the more reason to ask you kids for help."

"Help with what?" Olivia asks.

Angie places a glossy paper flyer on the table. "'Silverglen Street Party,'" I read. "'Food tastings, music, and more!'"

"That's this Saturday!" Olivia exclaims. "Where will it be?"

"Right here in the parking lot," Angie replies. "I'll be passing out smoothie samples, plus I have a few food trucks signed up as well. The rest is . . . more difficult."

"The rest?" I ask.

"The entertainment," Angie explains. "I have some giant speakers for music, but I'm not sure what else to organize. I'm too busy and not creative like you girls."

Olivia blushes at being called creative. I wag my eyebrows at London again.

London taps the flyer. "'*And more*,'" she reads. "That's what you need."

"More what?" I ask.

"That's the million-dollar question, isn't it? That's what I need help in," Angie says very seriously, like we're plotting some super-secret spy mission. "Are you in?"

London, of course, is immediately in. "We'll help you come up with awesome entertainment!" she gushes. "I know lots of people."

"What people?" I ask suspiciously.

"You'll see," London replies with a little smile. "Don't worry Angie, we'll help."

Angie smiles too, and her shoulders sag a little like she's dropped a huge burden. "Oh, thank you, London!"

London holds up a finger. "In return . . ."

Angie's smile slips. "Yes?"

Olivia and I look at London in alarm. Kids usually don't point fingers at adults and ask for things in return. I kick her under the table, but she moves away. “We don’t want payment,” I say.

“Not payment,” London agrees. “Maybe free smoothies or something?”

Olivia, Angie, and I all stare at her. Wow, *Shark Tank* has really made my best friend a tough negotiator.

Finally, Angie nods. “You girls do this right, and you’ll get free smoothies for life.”